THE RED HOUSE

GEORGE AGNEW CHAMBERLAIN

COMPLETE AND
UNABRIDGED

I

THE PINEYS used to hog the whole of the lozenge between the Shore Road and the White Horse Pike. But no longer is that region a mystery; too many thoroughfares have let in the light. Not so with the Barrens farther south, an irregular sweep of country that has defied unveiling for a hundred years. Highways have been bored across it, but step off them on either side and it is as though you had passed through a wall and closed a door behind you. Seen from the air, this area seems compact, an even blot of forest pierced by the oases of a dozen farms, each distant from the rest and solitary. But to a man on foot or on horse it has a diversity beyond belief. Bayous as sombrous as any in the Florida Everglades widen into creeks that narrow into runs. Marshes rise into sparsely wooded tablelands that plunge down unexpectedly into swales darkened by primeval trees.

No view anywhere, only discoveries. And roads. Roads that cross each other or intertwine or break at right angles for no reason. Roads that sometimes make a complete circle, like a lost dog. Roads linked to obsolete and forgotten treasure; this to a marl pit, that to a redstone quarry and another to a bog of buried cedar. Wood roads to rare sand, to vanished cranberry patches and even to faint earthworks thrown up as far back as the Revolution. Roads that tunnel through laurel twenty feet high. Obliterated roads, studded with young pines, that end nowhere. Still other roads, wide open, that tumble downward and cease in surprise at the edge of an impassable void.

Of the dozen oases, the most central and by far the deepest hidden was Yocum Farm. A plank house of eight-by-eight timbers mortised at the corners was the oldest of its buildings, and from this squat beginning had sprouted near by a huge barn, all the usual outhouses and eventually the main building. It was an irregular frame structure that faced open fields, but its rear hung over a deep tarn. The cleared acres were completely encircled by woods, billowing away or standing like a wall. Wherever there were hollows, the trees were mighty; elsewhere they had either the meager shanks of second-growth forest or the stiff flatness of scrub oak and jack pine. A lane with power wires tacked from tree to tree plunged westward for half a mile to the County Road, the nearest contact with the outer world.

The farm revolved around Pete Yocum, a hogshead of a man sixty-eight years old with barrels for legs. Everything about him was round, even his elbows and knees, yet nothing was soft. The white hair of his broad beard, mustache and head formed an electric nimbus that came alive to the least draft. Frequently, when about to speak, he would give a preliminary puff, and silky hair would shower out like a bursting milkweed pod. At sight of him, people were inclined to laugh, but only until they collided with eyes that created the illusion of a spider lurking in the center of a web. In a genial mood, the eyes might twinkle amiably, but anger could make them bore like gimlets or broaden into a defiant and terrifying glare. They had one more phase, occurring only at intervals, that would flatten them into fish scales. At such moments Pete turned purple and his vast bulk would heave with internal convulsions and threaten to burst.

Only Ellen, his twin sister, and Lottie knew the source of these attacks. Ellen was flat as a board, with faded hair drawn tight back over a well-formed head, yet for all her gaunt appearance she exuded kindliness. Lottie was her counterpart in build, but in nothing else. At first glance she seemed an ordinary colored woman until you noticed with a shock that her hair was straight and her eyes pale blue. Her son, Lot, was marked the same way. They were members of that mysterious people, the Moors of Delaware, and proud of the legend that they were descended from an Egyptian prince. Pete and Ellen had been nursed at the same breast with Lottie, making her a foster sister, twined into the web of Yocum Farm by a bond far tighter than wages.

Into this strange and hidden tangle of existence, fate tumbled a child named Meg Yarrow. Her mother had died in childbirth, and when her father followed five years later, Yocum Farm absorbed the orphan as a matter of course. From the start, her attitude toward Ellen and Lottie had been that of one more woman in a man's world. As for Pete, according to what mood he happened to be in, she soon learned to call him "Uncle" or "sir" or just plain "Pete"; in reality, he was her granduncle. He had been huge even as far back as 1932, the date of her arrival, an inexhaustible well of wonder. Occasionally he would scat her out, vexed by her unblinking gaze, and she would have to content herself with watching Big Alec, the capable farm hand, trying to pound sense into Lot's half-addled brain.

Surely no little girl ever fell into a cozier nest or woke to more sudden terror. It had happened long ago and at night, the hour between supper and bed. Pete sat in his great square chair that somehow always seemed a throne.

It had flat arms and a straight back with glides on its feet, so that he could shove it around at will. Without warning, his hands had locked tight over the head of his stout trench stick, armed with a pointed iron ferrule. His eyes flattened into fish scales and his bulk heaved and swelled to the verge of bursting. The cane clattered to the floor. His short arms reached upward and his fists closed tighter and tighter until they glistened like frozen snowballs.

"I'll tell the hull world!" he muttered in a strangled tone. "I will so!"

"Pete, be you crazy?" cried Ellen. "Pete!"

Then Pete's voice, strange and preceded by no warning puff, had resounded with a clang, "Drive right around! Drive right around and in!"

Ellen had ordered Meg up to her room with a rush, and never again had she been allowed to watch even a beginning of one of Pete's spells. The minute he showed the first sign, she would be hustled upstairs, but nobody realized how clearly she could hear Lottie falling on her bony knees to pray and Ellen's protesting cries, rising so high they smothered whatever Pete was trying to say. Suddenly he would snap out of it and let them lead him off to bed. Meg could hear that too. The creak of his chair. The pegging of his iron-shod stick, pitting the bare floor so it looked like smallpox. Finally, the groan of the big four-poster as it received his weight. Then silence, a silence more terrible than sound.

Even now, when she was sixteen, after such a scene she would creep to kneel at the window over the tarn and lean far out. She wasn't praying, like Lottie; she was running away. From what? That was the trouble; you couldn't say. Yet you felt something was loose in the house behind you.

Something you couldn't hear, see or name, that had been inside Pete, tormenting him, and now was out and free to roam. Though it never quite caught her, sometimes she almost wished it would, because then she could give it a name. Ellen knew its name, and so did Lottie; only they wouldn't tell. Just ask them about Pete's queer turns and why you felt this way, and their tongues and faces would freeze into stone.

Night can do a strange thing to you; it can shrivel you into a baby in your mind. But when morning breaks, you find you're quite grown-up and astonished to think you could have been so silly. Like this morning in May of 1943. Pete hadn't put on one of his shows for months, not even when he had lost Big Alec to the draft, and she ran downstairs to find him in the midst of a battle with Ellen.

Ordinarily, people noticed when Meg came into a room, even though there was nothing remarkable about her looks. Shoulder-long brown hair, seldom hidden by a hat, topped a neat body of average height that appeared to be featherweight, but could turn into lead when she anchored her feet. As to her face, one expression gave it one shape and another another. The same might be said of her eyes. From small and speckled, they could widen into pools of reddish-brown as lucent as the waters of the tarn. All her dresses were made by Ellen, and, strangely enough, they were becoming and sometimes even spicy, as if Ellen, while sewing, might have been listening to some echo from her own faraway youth. But looks were the least part of Meg. As if quicksilver ran in her veins instead of blood, she passed from light to shadow, not slowly, but swiftly as stepping across a line. Yet today Pete didn't notice her; he kept right on talking to Ellen.

"I've lived here all my days," he declared, "and no war ain't going to push me out."

"This war's different," said Ellen. "It's pushed plenty others out, folks with money behind them, outside folk with richer land than ourn. The paper tells how they're selling their stock and moving to town because of the loss of their boys or their hired help. Good farmers, too; men that's able to get around."

"You mocking my flesh?" asked Pete.

"No," said Ellen, "there's no call to mock it. It ain't your fault you can scarce move from wherever you're at."

"A man has two ways of getting around," said Pete; "one's his feet, t'other's his brain. My brain can walk faster'n any of them farmers you been reading about can run."

"Huh!" sniffed Ellen. "Then why don't you send your brain out to do the milking along of the rest of the chores, so Lot can get on with the plowing and planting?"

"There you go," said Pete, "reading my inner mind. That's just what I'm aiming to do." He swiveled his eyes until they took hold of Meg. "Meg, who's the huskiest lad in school?"

Meg thought fast. Johannath Storm was sturdy and by far the nicest boy, but he wasn't the huskiest; besides, she didn't know yet what old Pete was up to. "Reds Truman's son," she answered. "Teller, they call him, but he's dumb. Rising eighteen and he's only a sophomore at high."

"Dumbness won't hurt none," decided Pete. "If you'll fetch him out to see me no later than this afternoon, I'll give ye two bits in real money."

"I'll bring him," said Meg.

After breakfast she started for school. From the house, the lane swept wide of the fields to a drawgate, seldom closed. Then it turned sharp to the left, but should you face about, you could make out the masked entrance to an abandoned belt road that hugged the fences of Yocum Farm. Along all its length it was shrouded behind a tangled curtain of honeysuckle and greenbrier, and off it broke a fair maze of mysterious paths that dipped and spread through Oxhead Woods. But the lane she followed also held its share of mystery. Tightly enclosed by crowding laurel, holly and second-growth forest, it became a tunnel where silence was imprisoned. Here no screams could be heard; not on account of distance, but because sound couldn't get out. At the lane's end you didn't just reach the County Road, you burst into it, drew a long breath and perched on the milk-can platform to wait for the school bus.

How was she going to corner Teller? Though they had seen each other often enough, they were scarcely acquainted. He reminded her of the Yocum dog, Rumble, who lived on a chain under the apple tree at home, his eyes red with perpetual rage, his skin the color of sand, and under it you could see every move of his big bones and knotted muscles. Teller was like that, and the only chance she would have at him would be the lunch hour, when he would rather play softball than eat.

That gave her an idea, and when he came rushing out, she stepped in front of him and let him knock her down.

"My!" she exclaimed, scrambling to her feet. "My, but you're clumsy!"

"Me clumsy!" cried Teller wrathfully. "You buck into me blinder'n a scairt rabbit and it's me that's clumsy!"

"I know," said Meg with a sudden smile. "It was my fault. I did it on purpose because I wanted to ask you a favor."

He swept his eyes up and down her, and ended by trading

a leer for her smile. She made note that his sandy hair stood up in a brush between his big ears, for all the world like Rumble with his hackles raised.

"I guess you rate a favor," decided Teller. "Name it."

"Nothing much," she said. "It's for Pete Yocum out to the farm. He asked me to fetch you there this afternoon."

"Can't today," said Teller. "Maybe tomorrow."

Meg gave him a wide-eyed look tinged with sadness. "Sorry," she said. "Tomorrow won't do."

"Oh, all right," said Teller.

The County Road route had to be content with an improvised affair where the passengers sat facing each other, and during the ride Meg grew more and more uneasy over the way Teller would work his eyes from her feet to her knees and slowly up to her face. She left the bus sedately, but as soon as she was hidden from sight in the lane, she ran. She could outrun most boys, but not Teller. He caught up with her easily, seized her wrist and flipped her into the crook of his arm.

"Pay as you enter, sweetheart."

The tussle that followed taught Teller that an impact can be so sudden it has no beginning. Next came the realization that his notion of feminine frailty was a dud. Had he tangled with a girl or a full-grown coon? Whatever it was, its flesh was too solid to pinch and it had heels that were kin to a road scraper, to say nothing of several other cutting edges that threatened to leave his skin in shreds. He gave up all idea of a conquest by force and asked no more than to free himself. The only way he could do it was to hurl Meg off bodily. He did. She landed on her feet, pulled down her rucked dress and picked up her books.

"I guess that'll show you," she panted, "you big lug!"

"Aw, shucks," said Teller, looking her over admiringly, "all I wanted was a kiss."

"Better keep your kisses till somebody asks for them," said Meg, "even if you have to wait all your life."

She hurried along the lane, and didn't need to look over her shoulder to know that he was following, because once in a while she could hear a catlike footfall. Teller was bred to the woods; you could tell by the way he walked. He caught up with her only gradually, careful not to offend her again. Neither of them said a word until they came to the belt road.

"Ever foller that path and them it leads to?" he asked in the lingo he used outside of school, the only language fitting for a man.

"Not far," said Meg.

"I wouldn't if I was you," said Teller. "You'd ought to stay clear of timber tracts, specially Oxhead Woods. If I ever catch you west of the Yocum fence—oh, my! I'll pay you back, sister, and you'll pay me!"

Meg bit her lip, and when Rumble greeted them with a torrent of barks, thickening into growls that tore his throat, she eyed him speculatively. With a shrug of regret that his chain was so strong, she led the way into the kitchen and accosted Pete.

"Here's Teller Truman," she announced, "but you can keep your two bits. I want a dollar or nothing."

"Eh, eh," said Pete with a puff, "you'd think dollars growed thick as chinquapins. . . . Howdy, boy."

"Howdy," answered Teller.

He spoke absently because his eyes were skipping around like mad. It was hard to snatch them away from Pete and his puffing, the funniest sight on record, but there were other things to see. For years the Yocum place had carried a legend of opulence. Where else would you find a farm with an inside colored servant, working regular? Only she claimed she wasn't colored and there were folks who said the law backed her up, yet there she stood—black. She had the nerve to give him as good as he sent, a startling blue-eyed gaze as flat as a wall.

"By the looks of ye," said Pete, "you're a strong enough lad."

"I can lift a spoon as far as my mouth," admitted Teller with a grin.

"Be ye willing to work?" said Pete.

"What kind?" asked Teller.

"Nothing hefty," said Pete. "Just take the milk away from eighteen head, cool it, feed and set the barn to rights. Come after school and leave afore supper."

"How much?" asked Teller.

Pete's eyes contracted to their gimlet aspect. "Fifty cents a day," he said, "cash in hand."

The grin vanished from Teller's face; his upper lip curled in a sneer and his eyes turned red. "You ton o' beef," he muttered angrily, "who do you think I am? Kiss you and your fifty cents!" He started out, shouting over his shoulder, "Who's going to pay me my due of five bucks for walking five miles home? Me that wouldn't travel half around your belly for fifty cents!"

In an instant, rage transformed Pete's grotesque bulk into the threat of a toppling rock. His cheeks took on the dreaded purple tinge, but his eyes, instead of flattening into fish scales, seemed to spurt venom.

"Stop him!" he wheezed raucously. "Bring his greasy neck where I can squeeze it with only one hand! Stop him!"

Lottie let fly with a wire pan brush that almost tore off

Teller's ear as he kicked open the door and left. Outside, he snatched up a quarter-brick and hurled it at Rumble. It caught the dog full in the chest, and though it bounced off harmlessly, it came near to killing him anyway from choking to death with fury.

"Pete," murmured Ellen, "how fast did you say your brain can walk?"

Close to Pete's chair stood the sturdy three-legged stool which he carried with him whenever he went out. He gave it a petulant side kick, knocking it over. His chin dropped, causing his beard to spread like a baby's bib. A moment ago he had seemed a concentration of power, and even now he didn't look ridiculous, only sad. Meg felt sorry for him.

"Don't worry, Pete," she said softly. "Your brain was right, all right. Leave it to me and I'll prove it."

II

THAT NIGHT Meg lay awake, remembering Teller. He was mean and as tough as they come, but even so, it would have been a break to have him around, crashing like a bull into the hidden struggle at Yocum Farm and giving her something different to worry about. Then she thought of Johannath Storm, and when she woke she could hardly wait to get to school. Nath was barely seventeen and shorter than Teller's six feet, but stockier. The way a lot of the girls acted, especially Tibby Rinton, you'd think he must be good-looking, yet he wasn't—not really. He had freckles and rough hair, muskrat-brown, and when he smiled, his blue eyes would crinkle almost shut to the shape of a fingernail moon. Meg had never really talked to him the way Tibby

Rinton did every chance she got, but she had smiled at him more than once and he had smiled back. She caught him alone in the hall and walked close behind him.

"Nath," she whispered, "I'm in a terrible fix. Pete Yocum made me promise to bring you out to the farm this afternoon, and I just don't know what to say."

He slanted laughing eyes down at her. "You've said it all before you begin," he told her. "How long would it take?"

"Not so awful long," she said eagerly. "If you went out on the bus with me, afterwards you could cut across Oxhead Woods and get home right quick."

"Sure," said Nath. "I hadn't thought of that. I guess I can make it."

In the bus they sat side by side, and as they went up the lane together, she couldn't keep from thinking how different it was from walking with Teller. She spied Pete sitting on his stool in the open wagon shed, overseeing Lot grind feed.

"Here's another boy, Pete," she said, "a nicer one. His name's Johannath Storm, but everybody calls him Nath."

"Howdy," said Pete. "You ain't son to the widow that has the bitty crossroads store over to the Friesburg Pike, is you?"

"That's right," said Nath.

"I need a body to help me out with the evening chores," said Pete humbly. "You know what they be, good as me, and all I can pay is fifty cents a day."

Nath hesitated and might have refused if he hadn't chanced to glance at Meg. Her lips were half parted and the hope in her eyes changed her face so completely that it was like looking at somebody he didn't know.

"All right, Mr. Pete," he said. "I guess I'll take the job, for a while anyways."

Pete didn't attempt to hide his pleasure. "Well, now; that's right good news," he said softly. "Could you start today?"

"Sure," said Nath. "Just show me the lay of the place."

With an alacrity that made Nath gasp, Pete got off the stool, hung it on one arm like a bangle and headed for the barn. Meg went to the house to freshen up, and though Nath didn't need a lot of showing, Pete wouldn't leave him. He didn't say much, he just watched, and the longer he watched the deeper seemed his absorption with some fascinating project that made him think hard enough to raise a sweat. He had his cane gripped between his knees and was toying with a horseshoe, a big one. Nath wished he would go away. How could he work when his brain was teetering between thinking Pete was funny, yet perhaps he wasn't? Then Pete seized the horseshoe by the tips, straightened the cold iron into a rod, tossed it aside and spat at it languidly.

Nath felt his face turn white; now he knew whether Pete was funny or not. He didn't look at him any more; he worked hard, and presently he could murmur, "I guess that's all of it."

"Yes, sir," said Pete, "and you done right good." His hand started for his hip pocket, but stopped halfway. "You earned a bite of supper to boot. Come along in the house and set."

Because Yocum Farm had the allure of a walled castle that everybody knew about but few had entered, Nath was tempted. Besides, he wanted to have another look at Meg. It was queer how you could see a kid around at school for a couple of years and then discover she was somebody you didn't know at all. "I'd like to," he said, "but I can't. I guess my mother's wondering already where I'm at."

"That needn't worry ye," said Pete, leading the way toward the house. "I'll phone Mis' Storm soon as I git inside." He stopped at a pump at the end of an arbor that fused into the broad eaves of a lean-to whose roof swept upward to meet the clapboarded siding of the house. "Have yourself a wash; here's soap and I'll send out a towel."

Nath laid his jacket aside, stripped to the waist and stood laughing at Rumble, who was living up to his name; crouched on his belly, he looked and sounded like a maneless, grumbling lion. A broad grass-grown driveway broke sharply on the left into a steep-curving ramp, and at its foot, so unexpectedly close that it gave Nath a start, glistened the waters of the Yocum Farm tarn. Meg came running out with a towel.

"Better come over to meet Rumble before you wash," she said. Rumble hurled himself to the end of his chain, yelping and trying to jump on her. She pushed in his face with her open palm. "Shut up, you! Shut up! . . . Come on, Nath."

Nath crossed over and laid his hand on Rumble's head. The dog quivered, snuffling for the telltale scent of fear, but there was none, and without warning he rose and lapped Nath's face from ear to ear.

"Gee!" gasped Nath. "Half of me is washed already!" Meg laughed. She worked the pump while he sloshed the hay dust out of his hair and off his arms. "Some pond," he continued, with a nod toward the tarn. He tucked in his shirt and put on his jacket. "Deep?"

"You bet," said Meg. "But you'll find a path to the right that hugs the water all the way round until it meets the road through Oxhead Woods. Let's go in, Nath; it's getting sort of cold."

At Yocum Farm any meal was an event, but supper especially so. Heavy food was passed at midday, but along toward evening either Ellen or Lottie would get to fidgeting around the range, and, first thing you knew, delectable odors would start drifting through the house. Leek-and-potato soup has a fine smell to it, so have roasting spareribs, but perfume is the word for popovers. After perhaps only an apple and a piece of cake for lunch, Meg's mouth would get to watering so she couldn't speak without sputtering. But tonight topped all the suppers she could remember, with Nath so filled with wonderment that his eyes worked harder than his jaws.

Since the age of ten, he had hired out occasionally and seen a sight of farmhouses, but never any like this. An aura of abundance with Pete as its hub embraced the generous-sized logs alight in the big fireplace, and all the furniture was ponderous. Even the built-in corner cupboard was twice as big as ordinary, and Lottie, waiting on table, added an exotic note. She was imperturbable and strange, and gave him a sense of having invaded a foreign land. On the surface, everything seemed tranquil, yet he was troubled by a shadow. He happened to glance at Pete's pudgy little hands, and the shadow took on the form of a horseshoe slowly straightening.

"What's the matter, Nath?" asked Ellen with a smile. "Can't you eat?"

He colored and dug in, making up for lost time so fast that he finished as soon as Meg. At home he would have helped with the dishes, and it made him nervous just to sit around while one person did all the work. He felt he ought to go, but Pete hadn't paid him yet, and it seemed cheap to ask for a measly fifty cents. The sun had set, and as darkness billowed in from the eastern windows over the tarn, Lottie finished her work and left. Pete backed his chair well away from the table, and Ellen and Meg went to sit near the fire. Nath rose and stood uncertainly.

"Come take a seat, Nath," said Meg.

Perhaps she was wondering why he was hanging around, not knowing he hadn't received his pay. In the dimming light she seemed unlike any girl at all, a shadowy substance strangely illumined from within. He glanced at Pete and promptly forgot Meg. Sitting enthroned in his big chair at the outermost edge of the fire's glow, Pete appeared to be in the process of enlarging, as if he could make his great bulk swell out at will like a toad. That wasn't all. His gaze had an intensity that gave Nath the creeps. He decided he wouldn't bother about the fifty cents, and turned to go.

"Guess I better not," he said: "it's getting late."

Pete gave a labored puff, not his usual quick explosion. "Which way was you aiming to go, boy?" he asked.

"Why," said Nath, puzzled, "through Oxhead Woods, to save all of three miles."

"I wouldn't attempt it if I was you," said Pete, "no, sir. Shortest ain't always the quickest by a long shot."

Nath stood frowning, trying to figure what the old goat was driving at. What did it matter, anyway? "Guess that's right," he agreed. "Well, good night and thanks for the supper."

"Reckon you've never heard tell of the jumpity Red House," said Pete.

Nath stopped again. "What kind of house?" he asked.

"Jumpity," repeated Pete. "Set yourself down and I'll tell ye."

Ellen cast Pete a curious glance. "You'll do nothing of the sort," she said. "Let the boy go."

"Set," urged Pete softly, as though she hadn't spoken. "Later, you'll be right thankful I told ye the tale."

Nath sank tentatively on the edge of a chair. "All right," he said, "if it ain't too long."

"Forty-nine year ago," said Pete, "the Red House stood at the fork of Deep Tun in the depths of the Barrens, where it sprung from the soil a hundred year afore that. But it don't stand there no more."

"Well," said Nath, half rising, "I guess you'd better finish it tomorrow, Mr. Pete. I guess perhaps I'd better get going."

"Funny thing about that house," continued Pete, his eyes reaching out from the gloom as strong as two hands to push Nath back into his chair. "Lots of folks has seen it since it moved from where it was, the only house on record that has ever traveled up and down and across by night, looking for a man."

"But that's plumb crazy!" exclaimed Nath impatiently.

"Sounds so," admitted Pete. "But it wa'n't no big house and it's been seen in five places in the last forty-eight year to the certain knowledge of God-fearing men. Always by night and in some darksome hollow. Far apart as Frog Ocean or the sump that feeds into Millington Creek." He cleared his throat so sharply it gave everybody a scare, and spat toward the fireplace. "The house itself ain't much, but the screams that comes out of it, once heard, they anchors a man inside his flesh, piling the flesh on year by year."

Nath laughed out loud, more of a bark than a laugh. "Is that what happened to you, Mr. Pete?"

Across the semidarkness, Pete's little eyes broadened into a glare. "Yes, sir," he said, "it was."

A moment ago he had seemed funny, trying to make a scare out of growing fat. But now? What about the horseshoe? Had that been funny? Perhaps just flesh could become a prison stronger than walls of stone, and if Pete's bulk lay heavier on his soul than cross and crown of thorns, why shouldn't he pick on weight as the scariest curse of all?

"Shame on you, Pete," said Ellen, suddenly breaking into the silence. "Let the boy run along home."

"Why would I?" asked Pete sharply. "What have I got ag'in' Nath? So be he'll promise to go back by the County Road, well and good. But not through Oxhead Woods."

"Aw, why not?" said Nath, wondering to find his mouth dry.

"Because that's where it happened to me," said Pete, "no further from here than the middle of Oxhead Woods. Perhaps it's there again, perhaps it ain't. But if it is, the sound you'll hear will lay weight to your bones all the years of your life. Want I should tell you when and where to look?"

Nath glanced uneasily at Miss Ellen, hoping she might say something that would show up Pete for a fraud and shatter this foolish tensity with a cackle of laughter. But to his dismay, though she held no needles, Ellen's fingers were working as if she were knitting fast.

"Go ahead," said Nath loudly. "Tell me where to look."

"It would be after you pass the far end of the tarn," said Pete quietly, "the place where the bridge is broke and you have to jump across the black hole that once was the start of a raceway. Off to your right. There's a beech there so big it could shelter a flock of small houses easy as a hen covers her brood. It reaches over dark water, and the time I seen the Red House, it was floating on water thirty feet deep. Naturally, I knew the house wa'n't real, but the screams that comes out of it, they was real."

"Shut up, you old fool!" cried Ellen hoarsely. "Shut up!"

Nath went to the lean-to door, pulled it open boldly and started to slam it behind him, but he ended by closing it softly. He heard Meg call to him please to come back, but he kept on going, feeling his way through the dark. Outside, the moon was up, bathing the whole of Yocum Farm with mellow light. He turned to the left, but stopped at the pump where he had washed. The ramp seemed changed, as if it broke off short at the point where the moonlight ceased. Beyond was a pit of darkness, miles of darkness. He ordered his feet to get going, but they wouldn't. He saw Rumble sitting on his haunches and heard his tail swish, inviting friendship. He tried to whistle, and it frightened him to find he couldn't.

He knew he was acting like as big a fool as that yarning old man Yocum, but knowing didn't help. All the knowing in the world couldn't moisten his cracking lips or force his feet down the ramp. He turned the other way and found himself standing in the open where his eyes could sweep the circle of woods that enclosed Yocum Farm. Some of them were familiar, yet tonight they formed a forbidding, unbroken barrier around the lake of moonlight. Even the lane that tunneled through the stretch of growth between the drawgate and the County Road now seemed sealed with a plug of darkness.

Like letting a stubborn mule have his way, he gave up telling his feet where to go. They led him past the silent plank cabin and along to the wide entrance of the wagon shed. A gleam drew him, a gleam as golden as the rising sun. It came from a pile of last year's corn in one of the corncribs. He raised the sliding door of the crib, netted with strong rat wire, crawled inside and let the door fall behind him. He snuggled backward into the heap of corn for warmth, his aching legs sprawled wide. It wasn't only his legs that ached; it was the whole of him and above all else his heart. He had shrunk from manhood back into a little boy afraid of the dark. He was a coward. Tonight, only he knew it. Tomorrow Pete, Meg and the whole world would know.

Inside the house, Meg hadn't moved except to stare in unbelief at Ellen, down on her knees and with her face buried in her hands. Meg shuddered. This wasn't like Pete's ordinary bad times; it was worse, because it pushed her out and left her alone. Pete wasn't here, nor Ellen; she was alone with two people she didn't know. She saw Pete heave out of his chair and go to the telephone.

"Mis' Storm?" he said presently in his friendliest voice. "This be Pete Yocum again. Your boy et so much supper he's tuckered out and won't be home afore school-out tomorrer."

He hung up, and as he faced about, Meg found her tongue. "That's wicked," she said hoarsely. "Perhaps you did scare Nath into going the long way. But he's started, hasn't he? He'll get home hours from now and frighten his mother most to death."

"One fool at a time is enough," said Pete pleasantly. "Git ye off to bed, and Ellen too."

III

AT SUNRISE Pete went poking around in search of Nath. First he stopped at the plank cabin, but the boy wasn't there. He told Lot he could forget the home chores from now on, and ordered him to get to plowing. Leaving the cabin, he started for the barn, and it wasn't by accident that he caught sight of Nath in the corncrib, because Pete never saw anything by accident. Nath had been so cold that he had slept only by fits and starts, and his eyes were wide open.

"Hello," he said sheepishly.

"How'd ye come to get in there?" asked Pete, full of concern. "Somebody chase ye?"

"Only you," said Nath boldly. "You scared the hell out of me all right."

"Well, now," said Pete, "I'm sorry, Nath, and I don't understand it. Seems like the truth oughtn't never to scare nobody, boy or man."

Nath stood up, shook himself and gave Pete a long look. "The truth!" he muttered. "You and your jumpity house!"

"Eh? How's that now?"

"Aw, nothing," said Nath.

"Come along then; let's git them chores done afore breakfast."

Nath wondered if he was going to be rooked for double duty on single pay or perhaps no pay at all, but he didn't say anything—not yet. He worked fast, but couldn't keep from studying Pete at every chance. Perched on his stool,

Pete seemed wrapped in the benign innocence of an over-sized baby.

"Come here, boy," he said, the minute the work was done.

Squirming like a huge grub, he managed to extract a wallet from his hip pocket and took out an ancient dollar bill more than seven inches long and over three inches wide. "Here you be," he continued, "fifty cents for last night and fifty more for this morning. Come along in and feed."

Nath didn't follow at once; instead, he stood looking at Pete's receding back. There was nothing babyish about the old devil now. Why hadn't he handed over fifty cents last night? Had he planned the whole crazy show yesterday when he was thinking hard enough to raise a sweat? Nath felt so sore at being played for a dope that when he went inside to breakfast, he wasn't even embarrassed, and nobody else seemed to be either. Only Meg looked uneasy, her eyes resting solemnly on Pete. It made her angry to think he had known Nath wouldn't go home, angry and a little frightened. When she and Nath started off to school, their silence lasted well into the tunneled lane.

"Meg," said Nath, "does Pete often talk so crazy as last night?"

"No," said Meg. "I never heard such storying before from him or anybody else."

"Me neither," said Nath. He laughed and then frowned. "I was good and scared."

"So was I," said Meg. "When he got through, I wouldn't have stepped outside for anything, not for anything."

"Well," said Nath, "you notice I didn't get so far myself." Then he added, "But I will tonight."

They boarded the bus, and when it reached the school, Tibby Rinton was waiting. Nobody could belittle her beauty, with hair rising like an orange flame from the whitest skin you ever saw. But it wasn't white this morning and, since she never used rouge, only anger could account for the color in her cheeks. She didn't move; she just waited until they came near.

"You got a nerve, Nath Storm!" she exploded. "Where were you last night when I phoned, the way I said I would?"

"Working," said Nath.

"Working all night long!" gibed Tibby wrathfully.

"Aw, Tibby," protested Nath, "where's the harm? I did chores last night and again this morning. Can't a guy earn a dollar without you throwing sixteen hundred fits?"

"Not if it takes all night," said Tibby, turning away with a swirl.

After school Nath was torn between wanting to make it up with her and anxiety to see his mother. Tibby had been his girl from the first time she had called hello to him, and there were plenty of fellows ready and willing to take his place, yet when he remembered the chores waiting to be done at Yocum Farm, he decided to go straight home.

"Look, mom," he announced. "One of those funny old dollars."

Mrs. Storm was only thirty-four, but looked a lot older. Her husband had died when she was seventeen, and with the insurance money she had bought the little store and refurnished the living quarters in the rear. Up to lately, she had made a fair living for herself and Nath, but the war had knocked everything so topsy-turvy that now things were harder to get than to sell.

"It's a real dollar just the same," she said, smoothing out the bill. "Twice as much as the store took in today."

"For you," said Nath, "and I can get you more if you'll let me. Over to Yocum's."

"I know. Mr. Yocum phoned me twice; the last time to say you wouldn't be home."

"Did, eh?" said Nath with a scowl.

"Say, Nath, perhaps if you could stay steady over at Yocum's, it might be a good thing. Because that way I could go off to one of those high-paying war jobs and leave you fixed to finish school."

"I don't know," said Nath doubtfully; "it calls for thinking. Anyways, I got to beat it now, mom."

"Run along," she said. "But if you don't turn up tonight, remember I'll know why."

Twenty abandoned roads wander vaguely from the Friesburg Pike through Oxhead Woods, but only one ends at the Yocum Farm tarn. Nath knew he could find the way by day, but what about coming back after dark? He struck into the road he sought, moss-grown and hollowed out like a trough between banks from which sprang a tangle of laurel and holly. Arriving at a fork in reverse, he stopped to break a bush and bar the wrong way back. He did this several times, but twice he had to retrace his steps to correct a mistake. Abruptly he descended into a region where beeches, oaks and giant gums mingled their boughs high above the lesser growth so thickly that they blotted out the sky. The air turned dank, and a moment later he caught the gleam of water.

He noticed a strange indentation on the left, a sort of triangular trench that looked as if a plow had been dragged along on its side, only no plow could have passed through such thick cover. The next moment he came to a rotted bridge, jumped a ragged black hole and stopped, halted by a sudden recollection. He faced about, and there it was, just as Pete had said—no Red House, but a monster beech whose branches stretched across a pitch-black pool. The sight filled him with rage, and clawing up a clod, he hurled it at the pool. The water made a gulping sound and its widest oily ripple took on the look of a sardonic grin. He felt ashamed and hurried on. With startling suddenness, the narrow path widened into the flat platform at the base of the ramp. He didn't look for Meg or anybody else; he just went to the barn and got to work. Presently Pete came out with his stool and settled down.

"Late today," he remarked.

"Why wouldn't I be?" said Nath. "I had to go home first, didn't I?"

"So you did," said Pete, "but I'd forgot."

Nath gave him a steady look. "I came across Oxhead Woods."

"Did ye now?" said Pete blandly. "Sure, sure, that would be quickest—daytimes."

"Or any other time," said Nath with a short laugh.

"Think so?" said Pete. "Then happen you'd like to try staying to supper again."

"Sure would if I'm asked," said Nath promptly.

"So be it,'" said Peter, sliding off his stool.

As he toddled off, Nath had the feeling of having issued a challenge that had been glady accepted. He finished washed and passed into the kitchen, where Meg was seated near a window doing her homework. She seemed pleased to see him, but somehow surprised, as if she hadn't expected him to stay for supper. In everything except the variety of food, the meal took exactly the course of the evening before. When Lottie left the main house, Pete hitched back his chair and Ellen and Meg went to sit near the fire. But Meg looked worried, as if it distressed her that Nath should make no move to go. He stood with feet slightly straddled, a nervous smile tugging at his lips.

"Well, Mr. Pete," he said, "what about it?"

Pete eyed him up and down unsmilingly. "What about what?"

"That jumpity house you were telling about," said Nath. "Was it painted red or did it grow that way?"

Ellen raised her head and Meg gave a quick gasp. Pete alone showed no sign of surprise, but he was silent so long that Nath began to think he wasn't going to answer. When he did, his voice had the slithery sound of a snake rustling through grass.

"No, sir. Where would be the sense in painting Jersey redstone red? When you dig it out, like up to Burden Hill, it's so soft you can slice it with a knife, but air cures it same as smoke cures ham. The longer redstone stands the harder it turns, wax to the touch, but flint to the pick. That ain't all. It takes on more than the color of blood. It weds itself block to block and vein to vein. If you was to blow up one of them old stone houses, it would rise in one piece, fall in one piece and stay in one piece. Nor fire nor rust can't destroy 'em. I've known 'em to ring with the birth cries of generations, laugh with the voices of forgotten children and groans of uncounted dead."

"And scream," said Nath. "Don't forget the screams."

Again there was silence, one of those silences that turn doubly heavy for every second they last. Meg's lips fluttered as if she wanted to cry, but didn't dare. Ellen swayed backward and forward, her hands tight-locked in her lap. In the fitful light from the fire, Pete seemed not even to breathe. Night, rolling in through the eastern windows, packed the corners with tall shadows that took the shape of thugs itching to club the fire to death. Nath felt proud. He had called the old coot's bluff and now he could go. Straight across Oxhead Woods.

"Sit down." It was a whisper so low that for an instant it gave the illusion of having come from one of the tall shadows. Nath veered slowly, as if his head were being pulled around with strings. Pete's eyes laid hold of him. How could he ever have thought they were small? They bent his knees. They made him sit down.

"It was you mentioned screams," resumed Pete's whisper. Suddenly he hawked loudly and spat. It was as though he had fired a gun. Meg burst into tears, Ellen uttered a sharp cry and Nath felt sick because here was where he ought to laugh, and he couldn't. "Enough!" commanded Pete in his natural voice. "You women cease your caterwauling or git to bed and leave us men to talk."

Meg choked back her sobs; she was afraid to listen, yet more afraid of missing a word. Ellen straightened and gripped the arms of her chair; nobody was going to get her to move. Nath let the breath out of his aching lungs; he hadn't known he was holding it. Pete hitched himself forward and doubled his hands over the head of his cane.

"A Snell built the Red House," he said, "so far back there ain't no record. Snells has entered over its threshold and went out through the funeral door at the back since the beginning of local time. But until the coming of Hubert Snell, no question come up as to whether the Snells owned the house or the house owned them. Sounds unreasonable for a house to own a man, yet it ain't. Everybody can name houses as owns the folks inside. But the Red House went far beyond the likes of that. When it finished soaking up blood, it——"

Ellen stood up, her arms close to her sides and her fists so tight that the knuckles showed whiter than her face. "Pete," she begged in a rasping voice, "what for? Just to tie this boy to your side? Can't you hold him with the money instead? Can't you?"

"Like I was saying," continued Pete, as if she hadn't spoken, "it wa'n't me made mention of screams, boy; it was you done that. Howsomever, screams didn't rightly have no place in the stone houses of old, only the Red House. It takes years and years for screams to work their way through veins of stone, but once they settle, they settle good. It begun with this Hubert Snell. I can see him yet. I'm staring at him now. The thatch over his black eyes was so thick no falling rain could hit his face. A darksome thunderhead of a man that used lightning for spit. He had arms like a knotted cedar and a leg like the cedar's twisted trunk. Hube, they called him, Hube Snell."

Ellen's hands, slipping along the arms of her chair, made a sound like the squeaking of a tiny mouse as her body went back, her head farthest of all. With her eyes closed and her lips barely parted, she looked to be not of this world. For an instant Pete's gaze swerved to her, a quick look as sudden as a stab. Nath felt guilty; if it hadn't been for him, all this wouldn't be happening. He ought to do something to break it up, say something cheerful that would lift Ellen and all of them out of their trance. But it was Meg who blundered in to save Ellen.

"Is it Hubert does the screaming, Uncle Pete?" she asked.

"No," said Pete, "not Hube, though it's him the Red House is looking for. There's no question to it. Hube didn't own that house; it was it owned him, body and soul. For more'n forty year it's been searching for Hube, and seems God has ordained it must keep on till it finds him, knowing no rest. That's why it wanders from here to there, a lost house."

Nath was standing; a moment ago he had been sitting, and now he was standing without knowing how or when he had risen. He traded look for look with Pete, thinking he was being bold until he realized that he was doing exactly what Pete had intended him to do. Pete gave a puff, much harder than usual, and it made Meg jump inside without moving.

"Sure, boy, go out now if you're amind to," said Pete, shooting the words like spitballs. "Search the dark places, and not only Oxhead Woods. Search by night, and happen ye meet up with them screams, they'll mark ye once and forever. Yes, sir. Once heard, wherever found, you can come back to match your growth with mine, adding heft to heftiness, and only you and me will know why the voice that's raised in anguish can't be Hubert's, and never was."

He settled into his chair so smoothly that Nath was scarcely aware he had stirred until he saw that Pete's head was back as far as it would go and his eyes closed. Though he was so ponderous and Ellen so gaunt, the two of them had assumed an incredible sameness that made them twins in essence as well as by date of birth. As for Meg, her eyes looked like horse chestnuts, big ones, but without life. All three seemed fixed as waxworks, people you couldn't wake if you tried. Nath left them on tiptoe. He moved cautiously through the lean-to and reached the arbor. Clouds obscured the moon, creating a darkness that yielded to his expanding pupils only inch by inch.

But the stillness was worse than the dark. Even Rumble made no sound, though Nath could see the garnet glow of his open eyes. They seemed to be waiting for something, waiting for Nath to make up his mind, and that's what he was waiting for himself. All day long he had been planning to stay late at Yocum Farm and then cross boldly through Oxhead Woods. His manner had bragged to Pete and Ellen and Meg that that was what he intended to do. What would they think if he didn't? Yet he couldn't start. He tried to reason, reminding himself how old he was, one of the biggest boys in high, almost as big and old as Teller Truman. Would Teller draw back from any woods at night? The heck he would!

That did it. He started down the ramp, moving carefully, so he wouldn't slip and make a noise, never stopping to ask why he shouldn't make all the noise he liked. At the bottom, he had to feel around for the opening into the path that hugged the edge of the tarn, but once in it, there was no chance of getting lost short of the black hole. In spots, the path was firm, but occasionally he would strike a patch as slippery as grease. Alders swiped his face, showering him with dew. Lower down, his knees swished through hummock grass and wild roses that snatched at his levis with sharp little claws. Constantly the water on his left blinked up at him, and moment by moment the foliage overhead grew denser until darkness took on solidity, something you could cut out in blocks like ice. As he rounded a curve, his heart gave a leap and jammed in his throat.

Straight ahead rose a ghostly white column and seconds like ages passed before he recognized it for a shadbush in bloom. That was a laugh, wasn't it? Well then, why not laugh? Because he couldn't, because he was sneaking along as quiet as though he were trying to crawl up on a deer. How far had he come from the ramp? Half a mile? A mile? No, it couldn't be because——

Without warning, something heaved downward from the right. Ripping through greenbrier and honeysuckle, snapping alders like gunfire, something as big and hard as a boulder caromed against his shoulder and sent him headlong into the tarn. The icy water struck like a cleaver, severing reason from mind. Frantic with fright, he scuttled for the shore, climbed the bank and ran. He didn't need to see, feel or hear, for terror was a sure guide. It drove him back along the path and up the ramp. The big house loomed black with denial, but a gleam of light beckoned from the plank cabin. He plastered himself against its door, and a voice he had never heard tore out of his own throat, "Let me in! Let me in!"

IV

Lottie opened the door so promptly that Nath would have pitched on his face if she hadn't thrown out her arm. "Why, you's all wet!" she exclaimed. "How come, boy? Was you going too fast to make the turn?"

"N-n-no," chattered Nath, falling against her.

"Hush now," soothed Lottie as she started undoing the buttons of his jacket. "Let's us get you warm." She raised her voice. "Lot, come down here! Bring that winter blanket!"

Nath wasn't cold, but he was still too stricken to protest or even to notice that he was being stripped by a woman. He scarcely saw Lot emerge from a tiny corner stairway and was only vaguely aware of having a soft blanket envelop him from his neck to his naked feet. Only when he had been propped against pillows on Lottie's narrow bed could he rightly begin to take notice. There was a double light in the small room—a low glow from the open fire and a gleam from a lamp on the corner of the mantel. On a stand beside the bed lay an open Bible, showing why Lottie had been awake so late. He watched her drape his wet clothes on the backs of a couple of chairs close to the fire.

"How long d'you think they'll take to dry?" he managed to ask without stammering.

"All night," said Lottie, seating herself in a rocker so low that it lifted her knees level with her breast.

"Could you fix me up with something, so I could go home?" asked Nath, glancing speculatively at Lot.

"Where's home at?" said Lottie.

"Over to the Friesburg Pike."

"Unh-uh," grunted Lottie with a shake of her head. "Best get yourself good and warm where you be, then Lot can lug you up to Alec's old room topside the wagon house for the rest of the night. What happened, boy?"

"It ain't the cold got me," said Nath; "just plain skeer. I was going along the path, heading for the broken bridge, when something rushed down the bank too quick to see and knocked me head first into deep water."

"Oh-oh!" exclaimed Lottie, with a nervous glance toward the door.

" 'The Lord is thy keeper,' " declaimed Lot suddenly, " 'the Lord is thy shade upon thy right hand. The sun shall not smite thee by day, nor the moon by night!' "

He stopped as abruptly as he had begun, and Nath stared at him wonderingly. "I guess that's right," he murmured.

"Want I should read somewhat?" asked Lottie.

"Sure," said Nath, "go ahead."

She reached for the Bible and, using her slanted knees as a bookrest, she sought out a passage and began to read, " 'And I looked, and, behold, a whirlwind came out of the north, a great cloud, and a fire unfolding itself, and a brightness was about it, and out of the midst thereof as the color of amber, out of the midst of the fire.' " She peered at Nath anxiously. "It wasn't anything like that, was it?"

"Heck, no!" muttered Nath.

She started reading again, but before he could catch the sense of the words, they trailed off into a singsong and he slept. When he woke, he thought he must be dreaming, until he figured out the slant of the peaked roof. This must be Alec's room. His eyes traveled over the bed on which he lay, one chair, a washstand, a rough cupboard and a dozen wooden forks for clothes pegs, but his own things were nowhere in sight. A fine fix. Could he tend to the chores wrapped in only a blanket? He spied a pair of discarded overalls and was shaking the dust out of them when a black arm upholding a bundle appeared through the ladder hatch.

Nath took the bundle, and the arm vanished. Dressing did a queer thing to him; it restored his age. He was man-grown again, old enough to marry Tibby Rinton if he got the notion. Her folks were farmers and needed help worse than tomatoes call for sun. Perhaps it was his taking on work somewhere else that had made her so mad, but at the thought of chores he hurried down to the barn. Pete was nowhere around; he didn't even bother to come out. It was Meg who appeared just as Nath was finishing. Because it was Saturday, she had put on levis that matched his own, only a lot smaller around the waist. From there down she looked like a boy big enough to give you a tussle, but the minute he raised his eyes to her jersey and shoulder-length hair, she was all girl.

"Didn't think you'd hardly come back after last night," she said, "and I wouldn't have blamed you, not a bit."

He knew she was giving him a chance to lie, to say he had been home. He remembered he was grown, and started to tell her the truth, but stopped; there was something he had to find out first. He walked with her as far as the pump, then hung back. "You go along in," he said.

"Why, Nath," she exclaimed, "don't you want any breakfast?"

"Don't worry," he said; "I'll be back."

She watched him go slithering down the ramp and heard him turn to the right. Where was he going and what for? What if he was heading for home? The day stretched long and empty before her; she couldn't stand to have him leave her alone. She followed carefully, not wanting him to hear her coming, but she needn't have troubled, for already he was way out of sight. In the depths of the ravine, the bushes were still wet with dew and slapped her hands clammily. She thrust her fists into her pockets and hurried along, her sneakers making no sound. She had gone quite a way when she felt someone behind her, and turned. It was Teller, wearing nothing but a frayed pair of pants. The gash of his mouth was smiling, but his reddish eyes were dead as marbles.

"Didn't I warn ye to stay west of your boundary?" he asked softly.

"You don't own Oxhead Woods," said Meg boldly; "nobody knows who does."

"I'll show ye who owns 'em and you too," said Teller, taking a step forward.

He expected her to make a dash to get by, but instead she whirled and ran the other way. That pleased him fine and he didn't hurry; the farther she got from Yocum Farm, the better it would suit him. Never had Meg run faster, paying no heed to the alders that slashed her cheeks. Where was Nath? Could she hold out until she met him? She made a turn, and there he was, walking slowly toward her dangling a twig. If anything, she increased her speed and hurled herself against him, almost knocking him over.

"Nath!" she gasped. "Nath!"

That was all she could say in spite of the bewildered hang-jaw look on his face. He held her up with only one arm, because his other hand was guarding the twig, more than a foot long, from getting broken.

"For Pete's sake!" he grunted. "Say, what's the matter with you? Your heart's pounding fit to bust."

Waking to how close she was to him, she drew away, ashamed. "It's Teller Truman," she said. "He's chasing me."

"What of it?" said Nath. "You afraid of Teller?"

She didn't answer at once, only looking at him gravely.

"If it wasn't for you being here," she said slowly, "I'd be a lot worse than scared. I wouldn't have a chance."

Nath flushed. "Come along," he said; "I'll tend to him."

"What's the twig for?" she asked as she followed him.

"Never mind," said Nath. They heard a plunge and saw the V a muskrat makes when he crosses still water, only this was larger. "There he goes, low-tailing it for cover."

"But he was chasing me, Nath!" cried Meg. "Really he was! Don't you believe me?"

"Why wouldn't I?" said Nath. Presently he stopped. "So he was barefoot."

Nath knelt and measured one of Teller's footprints against a nick on the twig. "Short by an inch," he muttered.

Though the water was cold, Teller swam without effort, showing only half his rolling head. On the far side he seized the roots of a sour gum, but his feet couldn't find bottom. There are no stones in all that region, only pebbles, but originally the tarn had been a marl pit and along its edges there were chunks of clay as hard as rocks. He tore out a couple and climbed on the ridge of the abandoned raceway that paralleled the pond for a mile. Bracing himself, he left fly. The lump of marl, whizzing past Meg's ear, crashed against the bank behind her.

"Say," yelled Nath, "you crazy? You want to kill somebody?"

"Here's yours!" shouted Teller.

Nath saw what was coming, caught it like a baseball, took his time and threw. Teller was trapped; he couldn't dodge without losing his foothold. The jagged lump tore his shoulder and sent him over backward into the empty raceway, choked with brambles. Nath and Meg started on, followed by a stream of sputtering curses.

"Oh, Nath, it's all my fault!"

"Forget it," he muttered, looking down thoughtfully at the stick he still carried.

"Now won't you tell me what that's for?"

He told her the truth about getting knocked off the path the night before. "Of course it wasn't any boulder," he finished. "It had to be a man. This stick shows the measure of his foot, and it was bigger than Teller's."

"Then of course it couldn't be Pete's," said Meg.

Nath gave her a quick look that turned into one of his crinkly smiles. "Well, well," he murmured, "seems you and me sort of think alike." The smile faded into a frown. "Say, Meg, what goes on here at Yocum Farm anyways?"

She had been looking for him to ask just that, yet now she had no answer. "I don't know," she breathed.

The strangeness of her half whisper caught his ear. "So there is something."

Her eyes opened on him gratefully. "Yes, oh, yes! It's been here ever since I came."

"Why, weren't you born here?"

"No. I don't remember my mother and I was five when my father died. That's how long ago it began."

"What?"

"I can't name it; it's just here! Oh, Nath, don't think I'm crazy, please don't!"

"If you're crazy, I'm crazier," said Nath. "Look at last night and the night before. If I couldn't take it for just two nights, what about you—a girl, and a kid at that?"

"Kid, yourself!" said Meg hotly. "Huh, look who's calling who a kid!"

"Oh, oh, my! Where's the gray hairs?"

"I'm sixteen, only a year under Tibby Rinton."

Instantly she wished she hadn't mentioned Tibby, for she could see a change come over Nath. He frowned, thinking perhaps he was a fool to be getting tangled with Yocum Farm when a simple straightforward life was waiting for him elsewhere. Folks getting married as young as he and Tibby was nothing out of the way in that section; you could almost call it average; and when would times be better than now? With crops bringing fantastic prices and old man Rinton howling for help, he and his wife would do no picking and choosing when it came to grabbing a husky son-in-law.

"I'd ought to see Tibby today," he said; "anyways tonight."

Meg's lower lip started to tremble and she caught it between her teeth to make it behave. She felt the color rising into her cheeks. What would Nath think? That she was soft on him or something? Even her eyes were going wet, so how could she blame him? She faced him.

"Listen, Nath, go see Tibby all you like, if—if you'll only come back. Don't think I'm a softie, because it's nothing like that. Daytimes I'm not afraid of anything, not even Teller Truman, really, because the worst he could do would be to kill me. But there are nights that near shake the teeth out of my head."

"You mean that yarning of Pete's?"

"No, no!" she cried impatiently. "You were the start of that fool talk. Something else—something you'd have to see and hear to believe." They had reached the flat space at the base of the ramp and she pointed upward through the branches of a huge silver maple. "See that window?

That's my room, and sometimes I can't hardly keep from throwing myself into the tree just to get away."

Sunk into the hill on which stood the main dwelling and facing them was a small building whose wide doors, long unused, were laced across with vines.

"You'd be silly to jump," said Nath; "all you'd need do would be reach out for the nearest limb and climb down to the roof of this old icehouse."

"Is that what it is?" said Meg, disappointed and indifferent. "Anyways we don't use it any more, because I've never seen it opened even once."

Reaching the kitchen, they ran into a scolding from Ellen. "You're late," she said. "Lazy feet, no right to eat."

"Vittles don't figure none," said Pete; "what counts be the chores."

"Done an hour ago," said Nath.

He looked at Lottie, wondering if she had told, but her face was a mask. Pete paid him another dollar, and he and Meg sat down to eat. Meg was sad, realizing only now how cleverly Nath had steered clear of promising to stay around. When he rose, she had to hold herself down, trembling inside with wondering what he was going to do. He turned, and what he said to her was like an answer to prayer.

"I got to give this money to my mother, Meg. Want to come along?" They followed the narrow path in single file, but when they came to the broken bridge, he started looking for some way to get Meg across. Something brushed past him and she landed on the other side. "Say," he drawled, "that was some jump!"

She laughed back at him. "I figured if Pete could make it, I could."

Nath had to step back for a run to make the leap himself.

"Pete," he scoffed, "him and the cow that jumped over the moon!" Promptly, a vision of Pete's face rose before him, and the smile it wore had the shape of a horseshoe, slowly straightening. "Well, perhaps—so be that hole's been there all of fifty years."

The walk beneath the great trees had the dreamy feel of a trance. Bright young leaves were fighting the old ones on the laurel and here and there a shadbush was still in snowy bloom. In the roadway and folded over the banks on either side lay a blanket of moss that yielded like velvet to their silent feet. Nath was puzzled, because the triangular trench he had noticed had been obliterated and some of the bushes with which he had barred wrong forks had been kicked aside. As for Meg, she was too absorbed in contentment to think about anything very clearly, like sinking into a hot bath after a hard day. The world of trouble seemed far away and a strangeness fell on them, as though they were new to themselves as well as to each other. They walked side by side, companions on a journey, and nothing more.

When they reached the little store, it was shut tight, but Nath didn't seem surprised. He went around to the back and found the key and a note under an inverted flowerpot. In the letter his mother told him to look out for himself, because she had caught a ride to Wilmington and might stay on there if she found a good job; he could follow her or not, as he pleased. He gave the note to Meg to read and looked longingly down the pike, wanting to go straight into town in search of Tibby.

"Would you be scared to go home alone?" he asked.

"No," she lied promptly, her eyes steady.

"Well," he said, feeling he owed her more than thanks, "I'll be out later, same as usual."

Meg watched him hurry down the pike and around the first curve. She was no coward, yet she had no intention of going back through Oxhead Woods. Why ask for trouble? She dawdled along and presently a car offered her a lift. She refused, knowing that car would pick up Nath, but accepted from the next one. When she could see across open fields to the County Road, she asked to be put down. She was glad Nath had left her the way he had, because it had shamed him into promising to turn up at chore time.

V

Mrs. Rinton told Nath that Tibby had gone off on her bike in a bathing suit. It was too early in the year for swimming, except where the waters of a shallow lake got warmed by the sun. He knew the spot well and came on a group of girls engaged in starting their summer tan. Only little boys were with them, and his size made him feel awkward. The girls pretended not to see him, particularly Tibby. She was easily the pick of the lot. Her one-piece suit was of a green a tone darker than her eyes, and she sat in the shade because she had the sense to take her sun in driblets. The girls clucked and clacked, silly as pullets at feed time, and Nath was on the point of leaving, when Tibby got up and walked straight by him to her bike.

He took hold of one handle and helped her wheel it up the incline, waiting for her to speak, but she didn't. At the top of the rise, she mounted and zigzagged along beside him, her eyes as blank as if he weren't there. He grew stubborn; he guessed he could take it as long as she could, and they both held out until they reached the Rinton farm. Tibby disappeared to put on a dress, but her mother urged Nath to stay. At the stroke of twelve, Mr. Rinton and his sole remaining helper came in, their eyes sunk in their heads from work. Everybody sat down to eat, and throughout the meal not a word was said. But the silence was louder than speech, a sullen protest against leisure for any able-bodied hand.

Nath went out with the men; he couldn't do less. Some of the corn was getting its first tilling, but another field was ready to hill. He stripped to the waist and pitched in, but while he worked he kept thinking of Meg, wishing he hadn't left her to cross Oxhead Woods alone. If he had taken her home, probably he would have told Pete he was through; then he could have stayed here and worked until darkness brought an end to the day. As it was, he had to knock off at four, and he wouldn't have stopped at the house if Tibby hadn't run out. No blank look in her eyes now; they were full of concern.

"Nath, aren't you going to stay for supper?"

"Can't, Tibby. I promised to be back."

"Back where?"

"Over to Yocum's."

Color flared in her cheeks and her eyes blazed. "You go to Yocum's and you can stay there forever! Just try it! Stay your whole life!"

"Aw, Tibby, don't pull that line again," he begged. "You know you're the only one for me, and always will be, but I promised, honest I did."

"I guess perhaps something's happened to you, Nath

Storm," said Tibby more slowly, and the anger in her eyes hardened into a threat as she continued. "Go ahead to Yocum's if you want, but afterwards just don't you bother to come snooping around here, handing me what's left."

"It isn't like that at all," said Nath sadly.

"Then stay here and prove it."

"I can't," he repeated. "I promised."

He went down the lane, not even looking back to where she stood, fixed as a post with her doubled fists held close to her sides. For the minute he turned his back on her a strange thing happened to him; though Yocum Farm was miles away, it became more vivid than things near by. He walked with long strides, caught a ride along the County Road and arrived sooner than he had hoped. Meg had brought in the herd and Pete was seated on his stool beside the barn door. Though neither of them said a word, Nath was as conscious of their relief as if they had greeted him with cries of joy. Meg, still in levis, turned herself into a helper, and it gave Nath a start to see how expertly she could match her hidden strength against a heavy can. Pete waddled off to check up on Lot.

"I'm sorry I left you to come home alone," said Nath as he and Meg started toward the house.

"Oh, I didn't mind," she said airily.

She meant it—now. Her feet were light, and so was her heart; it floated around inside her, robbing her body of weight. Her happiness was greater, all the purer, because she didn't know why she was happy. It wasn't because it happened to be Johannath Storm who had come back. It was subtler than any individual, the nameless warm glow of not being alone. Always she had stood on one side of a wall, with everybody else on the other. Now Nath had joined her, and it was as if light had destroyed darkness.

"Say," said Nath, "I'm itching all over. Think it would kill me if I took a dip in the pond?"

"It didn't kill Teller," said Meg, "so why would it us?"

"You're out of it," said Nath promptly; "I haven't got my trunks."

"Keep on those pants," said Meg. "It would do them good."

Nath looked down. "Gee, they're awful, ain't they? But I wouldn't have anything else to put on."

"You'd think you'd bring over some of your things," said Meg impulsively, and regretted it when again she saw a change come over Nath.

"Yeah," he said slowly, "yeah."

He was being pulled three ways—Tibby, his mother in Wilmington, and Yocum Farm. Each opened a road, and it wasn't as if you could jump from one to another—once you'd made your choice, you'd have to say good-by to the other two. Only what was the rush? Did he have to choose this minute? He got Meg to fetch him a towel and a cake of soap. Behind the shelter of the icehouse, he plunged, scrambled out, soaped himself and plunged again. He hated to put on his grimy clothes, but there was no help for it; anyway, his jacket was clean and warm.

As soon as supper was over, he faced Pete frankly. "I guess I'll go home before it gets dark."

"Why, Nath," cried Meg, "with your mother gone?"

"Eh? How's that?" asked Pete. "Gone where?"

"To Wilmington," said Meg, "and perhaps she won't come back for weeks."

"Where'd you sleep last night, Nath?" asked Pete blandly.

"In the room over the wagon shed."

"Good," said Pete. "You can have that for yourn whenever it pleases you. Meg's right. Why go all the ways home to bunk by your lonesome? Ease yourself down and rest."

All was as it had been the night before, except that Lottie hung around in the shadows and showed no intention of leaving. The day had been long and hard, and Nath was tired. What harm if he stayed a little longer? Nought but the way people were placed—Ellen, Meg and himself grouped around the fire and Pete off at the side—reminded him of last night. Already that strange hour seemed far away, and he could scarcely believe that only two days had passed since he had first come to Yocum Farm. Somehow, this room had him by the throat. Or was it the room? He glanced at Pete, and promptly wished he hadn't. Sometimes people look through you and sometimes beyond, but Pete's eyes weren't like that. They nailed you down.

"Say, Nath," droned Pete, "you and Meg so young and all, fair carries me back to the day when Ellen and me was trapped by a falling window sash whilst stealing jam. Pinned belly down for the old man's strap, we was. Grunt and whang, grunt and whang, turn about on our two behinds."

"Pete!" protested Ellen, but a fleeting smile brightened her weathered face.

"There was later times," continued Pete, "when along of Lottie we'd race through the woods, stopping to gather chinquapins or trade stares with a six-prong buck. Where be them deer now? Gone from all the Barrens. Gone along of that other lass. Elspeth—Elspeth Drake."

"Pete," breathed Ellen, her eyes wandering anxiously toward Lottie in the shadows. "Please, Pete."

"Like a doe, Elspeth would come with the dawn," continued Pete, unheeding, "and she'd leave only with the setting of the sun. No other lass ever stepped so light or carried a heart more vast. Laughter was of her web and woof, scorning sound to make itself heard. Her face was a loveliness, needing no pattern of mouth or eye or jaw to tell its beauty to the world."

"Elspeth!" sobbed Ellen softly. "Oh, Elspeth!"

"Aye to that," said Pete. His voice took on a sharper edge. "Nath, Meg, I call on ye to look upon Ellen—not this slab of woe before you now, but a girl with hair like trailing smoke and the smoothness and strength of a hickory sprout. Elspeth, Lottie and me, we growed too tame for the Ellen of that day. In her pride, she would roam alone, farther, wider and fartherer yet, an itch inside her to meet the devil face to face and make him knuckle down." Pete's voice cracked to a high flat note. "Did he come? What form had he? Shall I tell?"

"No, no!" cried Ellen.

She sprang to her feet and looked wildly from Nath to Lottie and back again. Pete was swaying in his chair and seemed to swell. His eyes flattened into an unseeing gaze, and purple flooded dark through his white beard. A shout came out of him; loud and sudden it drowned the clatter of his falling stick as he raised the quivering snowballs of his doubled fists.

"Black were his brows as the cedar on the hill, and blacker the heart within. Bring me his throat! Who brought me his throat? Who?"

Lottie swept out of the shadows and fell on her knees

before him. Nath stood up, staring eyes above hanging jaw. Ellen saw him rise, flew at him, seized his shoulders and rushed him toward the lean-to. A blurred flurry dashed ahead of him—Meg on the run. Ellen propelled him through the door, slammed and bolted it. In the kitchen behind him rose an incredible bedlam—Lottie praying, Pete pouring out a torrent of asseveration and Ellen's voice rising higher and higher to throw up an impenetrable screen of sound against sound.

Nath found himself outside under the grape arbor with Meg cowering against him. His arm held her tight to his side, and again he felt the pounding of her heart; only this time his own was pounding harder still. They didn't speak; they listened as if their bodies had become welded together into a single monstrous ear. There was method in the din of battle inside the house, each voice at war with the others, but Ellen's keeping ahead by a desperately narrow margin. Then silence, followed by rustling footsteps accompanying the measured stab of Pete's cane. It was over. Meg crept against Nath, her hands groping for his shoulders.

"Nath," she whispered, "I'm afraid."

He had a feeling he couldn't describe—something between the pride of being put in command of a rescue squad and the ignominy of having a baby pushed into his arms to hold. He led Meg away from the black shadows of the house and the blacker tarn, out into the moonlight. They stood side by side, their hands lightly clasped. They weren't thinking of each other as boy and girl or any other way; it just happened that they had been caught in the same trap. From here they could measure its limits, letting their eyes encircle the barrier that had no break. They saw Lottie pass from the house into the plank cabin.

"Has that sort of shindig happened before?" asked Nath.

"Yes, every so often," said Meg.

"Ever ask Lottie what it's all about?"

"No, never."

"Let's," said Nath.

VI

INSIDE the plank house, Lottie urged them to sit and fussed around, lighting the lamp and stirring the fire into flame. She sat down in the low rocker and took the big Bible in her lap. "Want I should read?" she asked.

"No," said Nath. "We came in here because we're crazy to know what it's all about—that racket, with you praying, Pete shouting and Miss Ellen yelling her head off."

Lottie was silent, merely fixing him with her pale blue gaze. "For one who has come here so lately," she said deliberately, "you got a bold tongue."

" 'Ask, and it shall be given you,' " said Nath, giving her stare for stare; " 'seek, and ye shall find.' "

Trouble struck across Lottie's face, and she began to sway backward and forward. "Take the Word in vain," she said, "and vengeance will surely follow. But even so be you speak from the heart, it's not for you to strike water from the rock. No more for me."

"You mean there is something, but you won't tell?" said Nath. "Is that what you mean?"

"Last night I befriended you," flared Lottie, "so it gives you the right to beat me down in my own home!"

"Shucks," said Nath. "Somebody gets me to come to Yocum's, and I find three grown people old enough to of helped float the Ark scaring the living lights out of a girl since she was five years old. Perhaps it ain't my business, then again perhaps a thing like that is somebody else's business."

"Oh, Nath," cried Meg, more frightened than Lottie by his threat, "please don't talk that way to Lottie or anybody else! If you do, if you ever do, I'll be sorry you ever came here. I love Yocum Farm. I love Ellen and Lottie and Pete too. They've been good to me, always."

"I'll be dadgummed," said Nath. He smiled, his eyelids almost closing. "You get me in here to ask something, and now it's you tells me to shut up!"

"I didn't! It was you wanted to come in."

"Hush, now," said Lottie soothingly. A loud snore sounded from above. "That's Lot," she explained.

"Perhaps we ought to go," said Meg. "He worked awful hard today; we might wake him up."

"Pshaw, you couldn't," said Lottie. "Lot ain't so bright," she continued sadly. "He can't only not read, he can't learn. Happen it ain't his fault, the way he was conceived afar off in the year of tribulation."

"When was that?" asked Nath.

"Forty-eight year ago come winter," muttered Lottie, then her head went up and she gave Nath a quick, searching look.

"Where's his father?" asked Meg. "Did he——"

"No," said Lottie, finishing for her, "he didn't die, not so far as a body knows."

"What was his name?" said Meg, glad of the safe turn the talk had taken.

A blankness dawned and spread in Lottie's face. "I don't remember," she murmured. "Land o' me, think of that!

Happen it rises from the way men is made. Some of 'em you see but once, and they stays in your mind forever. But another you can marry, and first his face and then his name fades away to nothing, and all you got left is Lot and the wonder of where he comes from."

"What was the tribulation?" asked Nath. "Perhaps that's what put Lot's pappy's name out of your mind so quick."

Again Lottie slanted a quick glance at him. Her eye-lids fluttered and fell, and with her eyes closed, she became all colored. The folds of a black scarf, wound around her head like a turban, added to the impression, as did her voluminous cotton gown, belted high under her breast. On the surface she seemed somebody meant to be ordered around, but the longer you stared the surer you knew you were seeing only a hard shell with lips sealed as tight as a clam. No telling how long she would have taken to speak if she hadn't heard Ellen calling.

"You'd better run along," she said to Meg, then swung wide-open eyes on Nath. "You too."

Outside, he waited until he heard the house door close behind Meg. Under the apple tree he found an old ax handle, tucked it under his arm and went to pet Rumble. He fiddled with the strong harness snap on his collar and whispered, "Promise you'll come back?" The dog squirmed like a great worm, his tail thrashing eagerly. Nath undid the snap and went down the ramp with Rumble close at heel. He took no care to go silently, and perhaps because he was ready and asking for trouble, nothing happened. They came to the leap, dimly defined in the moonlight. He tossed the ax handle across, jumped and misjudged. Because he tripped on the farther edge and went headlong, the blow of a club that was meant for his head merely caught him across the shoulders. The next instant a snarling thunderbolt thudded into action beside him and a tangle of bodies went rolling into the brush.

The unseen battle that followed held the terror of mortal combat. A growling snuffle and the rasp of a man's grunts formed an undertone to the crackle of breaking branches. There was a terrific thrashing, and abruptly a grotesque specter swept into outline against a patch of sky. It was Rumble with legs sprawled. Two hands, locked in his collar, whirled him like an athlete throwing the hammer and let him fly. He crashed into the gap, crawled up the farther side and stoop whimpering. Nath heard footsteps rushing toward the great beech and a plunge into deep water where any good swimmer is more than a match for a dog. He picked up the ax handle and waved it at Rumble.

"Go home!" he called hoarsely. "Go home!"

He watched the dog limp away, turned and started for the store. What man could hurl sixty pounds twenty feet? Not Teller. He hurried along, paying no attention to what forks he took, yet burst into the pike not far from home. In the morning, after a bath, he packed a bag with all the clothes he owned. He couldn't have said at what moment he had decided to return to Yocum Farm to stay; somehow, during the last few hours, he had become transformed into a sober somebody with whom he hadn't had time to get acquainted. A little after sunup, arrived at the top of the ramp, he turned and looked back across Oxhead Woods. He had crossed it three times in as many days, yet on this Sunday morning it seemed more than ever to wear an impenetrable mask. Rumble came to him on three legs; he examined the other and decided it was only bruised. He tied the dog, tended the chores and went inside to breakfast.

"Howdy, everybody; I've moved into Alec's room."

"Good," said Pete. "I seen how you was carrying a bag."

Where and how had he seen, wondered Nath. Could the old puffball look through walls? Lottie wasn't around, and Ellen and Meg seemed odd in their Sunday clothes, Meg especially. After breakfast Lot came in and sat in a far corner. Presently he was followed by Lottie, carrying her Bible. She went straight to the head of the table, read a chapter, then sank on her knees and proceeded to pray. Everybody knelt except Pete, including Nath. He felt queer, braced on his elbows and staring at the back of his chair when he knew he ought to have his eyes closed. But soon he was welcoming the chance to think, to add up all the extraordinary happenings that had ended by tying him into a mess that was none of his business as tight as a fly in a spider web.

The prayer was long. It thanked God for a variety of blessings and exhorted Him to give proper attention to sinners in general. But when it took a turn toward particular cases, Ellen broke in with a sharp "Amen." She got up as if everything was over, and it was. Lot went out, and his mother after him. Pete was snoring as regularly as a dripping faucet; he had been asleep for the last five minutes. Nath wasn't the only one who had seized the chance to think things out; as soon as Meg got to her feet, she faced him.

"Say, Nath, let's go fetch Tibby." She turned to Ellen anxiously. "Couldn't we? Wouldn't it be all right to bring Tibby Rinton for Sunday dinner?"

"Of course," said Ellen. "Bring anybody you're a mind to."

"How?" said Nath, frowning.

"With Blackie in the surrey," said Meg eagerly. "Come on, I'll show you."

Blackie was so fat they could hardly get him between the shafts of a high-wheeled contraption reminiscent of the Dark Ages. They went down the lane, but before they reached the County Road, Meg gave a tug on the right rein and they turned into a grass-grown way Nath had never followed. It crossed a run, meandered through high trees for all of two miles and then climbed a crest. He stared down unbelievingly. Below was a swale he knew well, a low bridge, and beyond it the bars to the Rinton back pasture. Minutes later he was taking them down while Meg drove through.

Tibby hadn't gone to church, and when she heard the rumble of the bridge she stepped out to watch the strange approach. The hutch on wheels bordered the orchard and came to a stop at the barnyard gate. Meg jumped down, pushed through, and the two girls measured each other as Meg drew nearer. She felt awkward in her stiff best dress when Tibby looked so comfortable in a square-yoked play suit, socks and sneakers. But Tibby's lovely face was marred by a sulky look and her eyes were narrowed with wondering what on earth Meg wanted.

"Say, Tibby," said Meg a little breathlessly, "I'm awfully glad you're home. Won't you come over to Yocum's for Sunday dinner? Please do."

Tibby was taken by surprise, but the veiled fame of Yocum Farm had the same allure for her that it had had for Nath. "I don't know," she said doubtfully. "How would I get back?"

"I'll bring you," said Meg, "or if you stay till Nath is through with his chores, he could do it."

"All right," drawled Tibby. "But what would we do, all that time? Could we go swimming?"

"I guess so," said Meg; "only the water in our pond is awful cold."

"Anyway, we could lie in the sun," said Tibby. "I'll get my suit and leave a note."

Nath had turned the surrey around, quite a job for anybody accustomed to a car, and Meg made Tibby sit in the middle. The countryside was at its loveliest. Pear trees, at the end of their blooming, were sending out shoots of bronze; while apple blossoms blinked pink and red amid a blur of green. When they reached the woods, the sunlight, filtered through the tender foliage of spring, became an opalescent mist. They rode through it in silence, weighted down with the burden of life's confusion. The fat horse knew exactly where he was going—he was headed for home; but the best each one of them could do was to stare ahead and wonder. Nath: *Perhaps the war will last long enough to grab me, and I won't have to worry.* Tibby: *What is Meg Yarrow up to anyway?* Meg: *Why are they both so quiet? Can't they see I only don't want to be alone?*

Amid surrounding trees the tarn opened a funnel to the sky, and through it poured the sun. Half the platform at the base of the ramp was hot as a griddle, but a roll would take you into the shade of the big silver maple.

It was easy to tell why Tibby had been keen on pretending to go swimming. Green suit and greener eyes. The flame of her hair piled on her head, ready for the helmet she wouldn't put on. But above all else, her body—its sweep of line and precision of adolescent curve. In addition, after one look at Meg, she was at ease. Meg's skimpy skirt and halter were homemade, and there was a golden-brownish tinge to her arms and legs that made her look half tanned already; in no time you wouldn't be able to tell her from a tree or the brown earth. Nath looked funny in his trunks, because all of his neck and half his arms had a deep tan while the rest of him was almost as white as Tibby. When he went to crouch to test the water, both girls gave a gasp.

"Nath!" cried Tibby. "What on earth happened?"

"Why?" said Nath, turning in surprise. "What's the matter?"

"There's a black-and-blue streak across your back as big as a baseball bat. How'd you get it?"

"Oh, that," said Nath coloring. "I don't know."

"Of course you know." Tibby turned on Meg, who hadn't said a word. "And you do, too. How'd he get it?"

"I can't guess any better than you," said Meg.

"That's not true," said Tibby, ready to sob with rage. "Both of you know."

"I think you're horrid," said Meg, the brown blaze of her eyes transforming her face. "If it wasn't I had asked you to Sunday dinner, in about two minutes there'd be a new baldhead around here just about your size."

"Try it!" gulped Tibby, rising to her knees. "Just try it!"

"Aw, shut up, both of you," said Nath, seizing Tibby by an ankle. "Give me a chance and I'll tell you what happened. When I was going home last night somebody socked me across the back with a club."

"Home?" breathed Meg. "Did you go home?"

"Who? Where?" asked Tibby.

"Halfway across Oxhead Woods," said Nath, "but I don't know who."

"Was it Teller?" asked Meg.

"No, because Teller couldn't of done what this guy did. He slung Rumble all of twenty feet."

"Oh," said Meg, "so that's why he's holding up one foot and looking like he wanted to cry."

"He's not hurt bad," said Nath, rising. "Nothing's broke in him or me. Watch!"

He dived, and Meg followed him in, but the haste with which they scrambled out kept Tibby on shore. She loafed in the shade while they rolled in the sun, warming themselves. The three of them made a fancy picture, taking life so easy, but to somebody watching from across the water, only two of them counted. Teller Truman, crouched against the trunk of the sour gum, knew he was safe from sight, yet he could see out as well as through a telescope. Ever since the girls had first come down from the house, his bloodshot eyes had held them in such close focus that Nath's arrival had scarcely registered. Now Nath jumped up and seized Meg above the elbows, thinking to push her over the brink.

"In you go!"

"No!"

She anchored her feet and stood firm as a post, letting her weight sag backward. He laughed and pushed harder. Presently he was straining, his face red from exertion and the feel of Tibby's mocking eyes. Without warning, Meg threw back her hands, locked them around his neck and ducked. Leverage and timing were perfect. He described an arc through the air and fell on his back in the water with a great splash.

Tibby laughed, swaying from side to side from her hips up. Her anger at Meg passed as quickly as it had flared, and she was glad when Lottie called down that it was time to eat. What food! But Tibby was so entranced by Pete that twice her fork missed its way to her mouth. As for Pete, he wasn't at all himself. The first sight of Tibby had struck him dumb, not only silencing his tongue but anchoring his senses in a stillness as dead as wax. Only his eyes had life without movement, holding her image within their flood while deep inside his bulk his heart echoed the name of Elspeth Drake. He kept so still that he seemed to be absent, and after dinner the three young folk, ignoring him, went out under the apple tree to make a fuss over Rumble. That didn't last long, and a nervous silence fell on them. Hands in his pockets, Nath started scuffling the ground with his toe.

"Why don't you show Tibby around, Nath?" said Meg. "There's Lottie's funny old house and the barn and Alec's room."

"Who's Alec?" asked Tibby.

"He's gone," said Nath. "The room he had is where I sleep, but you'd have to climb a ladder to see it."

He and Tibby wandered off, and Meg didn't mind their not asking her to go along, because this was the way she had meant it to be. It was a mixture of instinct and shrewdness that had led her to pick on Tibby as the greatest threat to Nath's staying on at Yocum Farm. What was the answer? Simple enough. Fix it so Tibby would like to have him stay. Little things like showing her a good time, making her welcome whenever she chose to visit and letting her know from the start that Nath didn't sleep in the house. Above all, making her realize nobody was trying to steal her date, only wanting to have him around.

Meg changed into her damp bathing suit and ran down the ramp to where a patch of sun lingered at the very verge of the platform. She lay in it, face down, and was just about to turn over and toast her front when a voice—not loud, more like somebody skipping a stone straight to a mark—came zipping across the tarn. "Hi, mushie! Now's our chance to take a walk. Try it! Meet me at the race-way's end and I'll treat ye to a kiss!"

Meg felt her muscles tense one by one, and very slowly she lifted her face toward the sound. "Mushie" was short for "muskrat," and her brain seethed with trying to think of something bad enough to call back. At what? All she could see was the trailing branches of the sour gum; beneath and beyond that curtain there was only the somber blackness of Oxhead Woods.

VII

THERE is no season the like of May, be it a month of the year or a time of life. Seeds stir in the ground, sap boils, dogwood spreads its shining sheets and young people dream. They shed their winter thoughts with their winter clothes and match their brightness to the brightness of the budding world. Fear hides its face, running away from laughter. Blood takes on strength and paints lip and cheek with its flow. But surging against the rock of wonder in a young eye, it can ebb faster than any tide, leaving a pallor in its wake. Hot and cold. Up and down. Long and short. May.

Tibby came to Yocum Farm almost as often as had that Elspeth of long ago. She had known from the start, because of Pete's reaction, that there was no danger of wearing out her welcome. Her first appearance had been a shock to him, as if a ghost had entered the room. But soon he grew used to watching her startling loveliness pack away a full meal, proving she was alive and real. He didn't care to talk to her particularly and still less to hear her talk. It was enough to see her around, and at such times a mellowness would come over him, an inner radiance so powerful that it made him glow like a lamp. It was a pleasant thing to have happen, a little puzzling to Meg and Nath, but so clear to Ellen and Lottie that sometimes they, too, would grow strangely absent.

Mrs. Storm wrote that her days were divided between hard work and harder sleep, and when June brought the closing of school, Nath went on full time—six dollars a week and board. He could have earned double that elsewhere, as Tibby kept telling him, but he wouldn't leave. Something was holding him—something he couldn't explain to her and only vaguely to himself. Meg had nothing to do with it; even Tibby grew willing to admit the truth of that. What held him was a mixture of pride and curiosity so tangled into his own growth that he couldn't have cleared out without tearing away a bit of himself. There was something more; instinctively he shrank from the shame of admitting that the mere air of a place could lick him.

On all Yocum Farm, nobody was happier than Meg, full of the elation of accomplishment. Hadn't she succeeded in making her world over to the pattern of a dream? No longer was she alone. Even if Pete, Ellen and Lottie should put on one of their terrifying shows, banishing her to her room, she knew what she would do—climb down through the silver maple and go in search of Nath. He was at hand day and night, and it was she who had fixed it that way. Tibby Rinton too. Hadn't her cleverness used Tibby the same as a worm to catch a fish? Only Tibby wasn't really a worm. As long as she could feel that Nath was her private property, she was good-natured and friendly in her lazy way. Besides, look what just the sight of her could do to Pete. Finally, there was comfort in the fact that Nath had precious little time for fooling around with anybody.

By dark on weekdays he was dog-tired and ready for bed, and on Saturday evenings he dreaded the trip into town to take Tibby out to dance or to a picture. Tibby sensed it, and it wasn't long before she was glad to trade any Saturday night for Sunday at the farm, with Nath bucked up by a full night's sleep. She would arrive early and wait around until Lottie had got through holding church before she went in to say howdy to everybody, especially Pete. Then she, Meg and Nath would race for the barn and hitch Blackie to an old spring wagon. All it had for a seat was a board, and Tibby always sat in the middle. Meg didn't mind, because only she and Nath knew the true nature of the game they were playing. A good name for it would be: Looking for the Red House. It was Nath's secret and hers. They hadn't planned or talked about it; it had just happened, a spontaneous rebellion against their past fears.

There is a saint for every day in the year, and it seemed each one of them could have stood patron to a separate road in the Barrens. Only a dozen started from Yocum Farm in one direction or another, but eventually these would run into or cross all the rest. With such a variety to pick from, it was easy to find new sights and still easier to get lost. More than one excursion ended with a cold reception back home and a colder dinner. But a day came that gave Nath and Meg more to worry about than cold food. They had turned and twisted and gone back and forth; then never back again. At the moment that a swale diverted

Nath's and Meg's attention, making them wonder if it was one of those treacherous peat bogs that can smirk like a puddle, yet swallow a horse, Tibby let out a cry, "Look!"

They did. They raised their eyes and beheld a stone house, pinkish red. It looked like an excrescence of the soil itself, as if the knoll on which it stood had sprouted a wen. Its shuttered windows were blind, its sealed door seemed a scab and its shingled roof a forest of lichens and mold. It was small, dwarfed by trees that weren't even big, yet the shock of finding it at last was so great that Blackie sensed their dismay by contagion. He whirled of his own accord, rasping the wheel with a loud screech, and broke into a trot. Nath let him go, both he and Meg too bemused to mark the way they went. That day they really got lost, and only by leaving it to Blackie did they manage to reach home before dark.

Not only Ellen and Lottie were cross. Pete felt that he had been cheated, keeping him awake for hours with waiting for his weekly orgy with the past. As for Tibby, she couldn't understand what had come over Nath and Meg, turning them deaf and blind with their eyes wide open. She ate in a hurry, murmured her thanks and left. Nath followed her out and suggested he walk beside her as far as the County Road. Without bothering to answer, she hopped on her bike and was off. He watched her become a blur in the twilight before he went to the wagon shed, climbed the ladder and threw himself on the bed.

Tibby was blotted from his mind, and in her stead stood the Red House. Why had he permitted Blackie to leave the spot so quickly? Was it because he was in just as much of a hurry to get out of there himself? He felt ashamed, and two nights of wondering was all he could stand. Meg made it worse, staring at him at every chance, but never saying a word. On Tuesday he knocked off at four, summoned her with a nod, and together they made their first try to go back. What for? To make sure of what their eyes had seen. Just to find the house again. Perhaps to pound on its door, break it open and let in light.

They didn't find it on that afternoon or any other of the week; even the whole of Sunday, with Tibby along to help remember the maze of forgotten turns, couldn't bring them to that swale again. The effect of the vain search was more marked on Nath than on Meg. To her, the glimpse of the Red House stood for justification of all she had done. It had been real, hadn't it? Not just a fiction of Pete's crazy imagination. So it made him real, too, vindicating all her fears, and mentally she proceeded to consign herself to Nath's care with a contented sigh. Her attitude reminded him of when he had stood between the pride of heading a rescue squad and the ignominy of having been handed a baby to hold, only this was a lot more serious. They didn't talk, least of all with Tibby around; they just felt, and Nath took to wearing a constant frown.

"What's the matter with you two?" demanded Tibby angrily. "You just sit there, chewing gloom for gum by the hour. Can't you smile once a day? Can't you even spit?"

Meg was alarmed. "Nath's got the bee," she explained hurriedly, "because he can't find that old house. That's the way he is. When he forgets where he left something, he just has to find it or bust. . . . Don't you, Nath?"

"Listen who's telling me about the way he is!" exploded Tibby. "Who do you think you are? His grandma?"

"Aw, Tibby, please," said Meg. "I didn't mean a thing,

and you know it. All I did was tell you what's the matter with Nath and me too."

"I don't see as it's helped a lot," said Tibby. "Look at him! First he couldn't speak and now he can't hear. Where's the cat, Nath?"

"What cat?" asked Nath.

"Oh, so she didn't eat your tongue; she just borrowed it!"

Nath turned toward her, and his eyes crinkled slowly. "Gee, Tibby, you're a swell-looker. When you're mad I guess perhaps you're the swellest-looker there is anywheres."

The praise mollified her, at least for the time being, and the next Sunday prolonged the truce. Morning opened with rain, and it kept on raining. Wind too. The branches of the silver maple, whipping against Meg's window, woke her, and at first she was depressed, realizing that there would be no Tibby and no roaming through the woods on such a day. She remembered Nath's presence and was cheered. But perhaps he might go to town anyway, and again her heart sank, lower than ever. She kept an eye on him all through breakfast, saying nothing, just hoping.

Lottie went through her church act as usual, but when she and Lot started to leave, the briskness of the downpour drove them back. For a moment, Nath stood at the window, studying the flooded lane, and Meg held her breath. He sat down and, happening to look at her, was astonished to see color leap to her dusky cheeks, lighting up her face and her eyes. He remembered his first day at Yocum Farm and how she had changed from one thing to another so fast that you couldn't keep track. Now she was at it again. After weeks of being as easy as an old shoe, here she was flaming into a brush fire for no reason at all. It troubled him. People had a right to stay put in your mind, like Tibby. He thought perhaps he had better try to get to town, after all, but at that moment came a gust that fairly shook the house, and with it a great slosh of rain. Pete wore a lost look; for the third Sunday running he had been robbed of his visual reminder.

"The rain down Ellen's cheeks!" he cried out dolefully. Everybody looked quickly at Ellen and then at him. Immediately it became plain that he was far from the room, long years away. "Elspeth was loveliness," continued memory's voice, "but Ellen was strength. Early to bed was her motto. Aye, early, but not to bed. Down the silver maple as smooth as a whip snake, down and off through the night. Pride was in her feet, in the spring of her thighs and in her laughter. But tears poured down like rain when she came back. Aye, roaming lass! Didst thou think to draw out leviathan with a hook or bore his jaw through with a thorn?"

Lot's bowed head flew up, and seizing the seat of his chair, he leaned forward with staring eyes. "Leviathan!" he croaked hoarsely. " 'Who can open the doors of his face? His teeth are terrible round about. His scales are his pride.' "

"Shut up, you!" said Lottie sharply. "Get along out of here!"

Lot's body writhed, but his hands held him down. " 'Out of his nostrils goeth smoke, as out of a seething pot or caldron. His breath kindleth coals.' "

"You, Lot!" shrilled Lottie. "Take yourself away! You hear me?"

Lot rose and groped for the door, wall-eyed with staring at the unseen. " 'The flakes of his flesh are joined together . . . they cannot be moved,' " he groaned. " 'His heart is as firm as a stone; yea, as hard as a piece of the nether millstone.' "

"Aye, aye, that's him!" cried Pete. "That's him that Ellen found! Up she went and down she went, turn here and turn there, follering the call of the Red House. The little house, red by night as a boil is red in the sun by day! A wart on a knoll! The comb on a bald-headed rooster! Two yellow windows below for ears and two above for eyes, and a door for its black mouth! Did she rap with her knuckles? Oh, no! A laugh was her knocker, and the door opened wide."

Ellen rose, sadness and dignity in her face. She stood with her back to Pete and looked from Nath to Meg and back again. "Into such a rain," she said quietly, "you can't go out. And though the house be large, sound travels through it like water through a mill. All I can ask is, out of kindness stop your ears."

Meg's heart piled into her throat as she sprang to her feet. "Come on, Nath!" she gulped. "Let's make a run for Lottie's cabin."

Nothing could have suited Nath better. So great was their haste that he and Meg collided in the doorway, but passing through the lean-to, he had the sense to snatch a raincoat from a peg and throw it about her. To clamp the coat against the power of the wind, he locked one arm around her knees, the other across her back and doubled her over his shoulder. She was small but solid, a firmness to her flesh that nothing could break. Why had he worried about what water could do to her? Feeling foolish, he dumped her too carelessly on the bench in the plank house.

"Say, who gave you leave to throw me around?" she spluttered furiously. "Who gave you leave to pick me up?"

"Of all the brass!" muttered Nath, brushing water off his

knees. "You're welcome, Miss Yarrow; no trouble at all, so don't bother to thank me. Only I wish I'd rolled you in the mud!"

Meg had to laugh, but cut it short. "Oh," she cried, "you're all wet! You're awful wet!"

"Sure," said Nath. "You didn't notice, but it's raining."

Lottie came in with a gust of the storm, her voluminous skirt shamelessly bundled in her arms. She let it fall to slam the door and bar it. "That'll stop its banshee howl," she explained.

"Don't you think you ought to change your clothes?" asked Meg. "Nath could go up in Lot's room."

"Pshaw, no," said Lottie. "Only my legs is much wet, and that won't hurt none. I'll make us a fire and show you somewhat." Presently she produced a pack of cards, much used, and an ancient inlaid cribbage board with metal pegs. "Older'n time," she said proudly.

"Oh, Lottie," exclaimed Meg. "Cards on Sunday?"

"Well," said Lottie, "they's such a thing as playing fair. The Lord could easy have chose any day but this to send such a passel of rain, muxing up the peace of His own Sabbath Day."

The plank cabin had an intimacy unknown to larger houses. There was the nearness of the crackling fire, the little bench for a card table and Meg and Nath in low chairs, so close that their knees had to touch. The storm's rage seemed to rise to fury because it found the cabin too hard a nut to crack. Lot crept down for company. Nath couldn't keep his mind on the cards and quit in the middle of a game.

"Lottie," he said, "it's two weeks ago today Meg and me came on the Red House, but we haven't been able to find it since. To anybody that'll show us the way back, I'd gladly hand over a week's pay." Lottie gave him a stony stare. "Aw, where's the harm?" continued Nath. "Would it be telling any secrets just to say what road to take and where to turn?" Lottie kept on staring. "What about you, Lot?" asked Nath. "Know where he is? How'd you like to earn six bucks? Find me the Red House and the cash is yours."

Lottie's face seemed to split in a cackle. "Sure," she said, "ask Lot, him as wasn't born when the Red House closed in on itself and never opened a crack again! What does Lot know? Nothing about nothing." She started rocking back and forth. "Only had it been across the river," she muttered, "where the whip is paid with the whip!" Abruptly she seemed to wake up angry. She sprang to her feet, picked up the raincoat and threw it at Nath. "You and Meg get out of here."

Barely an hour had passed since they had left the main house, and they found the kitchen quiet, but today it seemed too big for genuine peace. It didn't draw people together; it shoved them apart. Pete, snoozing in his big chair, stood for a county to itself. Ellen, calmly sewing on a dress near the fireplace, made another. As for the near-by parlor, never used, and the rooms above, they might have been foreign states. To Nath, everything stood for division, with even Meg off in a world of her own. He hadn't carried her back; the two of them had crowded under the raincoat, and he still held it. Now he put it on, borrowed one of Pete's old hats without asking, and presently went sloshing down the lane.

VIII

MEG climbed to her room to lie down; there was nothing else to do. Her bed was a four-poster, not heavy, but with strength in its delicate spindles. The canopy of white muslin wasn't flat; it arched lengthwise, and looking up at it gave you the feeling of being under a boat that was floating upside down. On the verge of drowsing, she seemed to wake to the call of words, tapping on the door of recollection: "Aye, early, but not to bed. Down the silver maple as smooth as a whip snake." She rose on her pillow and stared at the window. The great tree was waving like mad, gesturing, beckoning, and no doubt it was tossing its head. It was talking to her, yelling at her.

She threw herself back and closed her eyes as if it wasn't fair to see and hear, but she couldn't stop her mind. Inside it, two Ellens fought one against the other. Gradually, the familiar and beloved Ellen she had left downstairs, gray, flat and strong as a weathered-oak plank, began to blur. In her stead bloomed a laughing triumphant girl with hair like trailing smoke. Lovely, strong, incredibly young. Oh, oh! This must have been her room. From here she had climbed down and gone to the Red House. She hadn't needed any horse and wagon; she had gone by night and on foot. A branch of the tree swept across the window and flung toward the south: "Come on! This way! I'll show you!"

What was rain? Was it any wetter than the water of the tern? Meg rose and stripped to the skin. All she put on was a shirt, levis, socks and sneakers. Soundlessly she raised the window and caught the waving branch. It wasn't strong enough to hold her, but using it like a rope, she dragged a thick enough limb within reach, took a firm grip and let it swing her out. She gasped, half with the thrill and half because she realized she couldn't get back, not even to close the window. But that part didn't matter; blanketed by the tree, only a few drops would enter the room. She made her way to the main trunk and then from fork to fork until she could drop on the roof of the ice-house and slide to the ground.

She had her choice between the path along the edge of the tarn and an abandoned road that followed the boundary fence to the south. She chose the road because it was so choked with growth that it had never occurred to Nath to attempt to thread it with horse and wagon. The rain at her back scarcely bothered her, for overhead was a leafy roof of many layers while on her right hung a thick tangle of greenbrier and lesser vines. On the left, the lush underbrush formed another wall before it plunged downward into impenetrable gloom. Drops of water spangled her helmet of hair and only gradually soaked her clothes until they clung to her like a second skin. The air had the invigorating tang of wine; she was glad she had come and that nobody knew she was out. For once she was alone without feeling lonely.

The stake-and-rider fence staggered to a fat corner post buried in poison ivy, and there turned a right angle. The road neither followed nor did it exactly end; it fanned out into three trails, one as faint as the others. She decided to try them all, the westernmost branch first. But it faded into nothing so soon that it seemed a waste of time to go back; surely she could strike through the woods to the middle one of the three trails. Instead, to her surprise, she broke into quite an open road running at an unexpected slant. She couldn't resist the temptation to follow it around two or three turns before she decided she had better retrace her steps. At what spot had she stepped out of the woods? It was silly, but she couldn't find it. Not a footmark, not a broken twig, an unbelievable sameness. Panic touched her heart , but it quickly yielded to reason. What difference did it make which way she went? This road had to lead somewhere, didn't it? With quickened pace, she traveled in the direction she happened to be facing.

Time and distance lost their meaning, and she couldn't have made a guess at how long she had been following the strange road when it began to assume a familiarity as blurred as a half-forgotten dream. The conviction that she had been here before, and only once, struck weight from her feet, and she broke into a run, flinging her eyes to right and left at every turn. Abruptly she stopped with her heart in her throat. Down a short vista stood the Red House, not face to face with her as on that other day, but at an angle and across a tiny pond. The blood raced in her veins and her lungs filled to bursting. She threw back her head and a clear young laugh went ringing into the silent woods.

Not through the door of the house, but from around back of it, broke a figure so grotesque that she didn't recognize it at once for a man. He came toward her with long loping strides that enlarged him fantastically. Out of his woolen shirt and rolled trousers protruded arms and legs almost as hairy as his orange-tinted head. The same fiery growth covered his jowls, and only when she woke to the blaze of fury in his yellow eyes did she realize how rapidly he was drawing near. She felt an instant of despair, a premonition of mortal danger. In how many strides could he cross the pond? But he knew that sinkhole better than she, and swerved to go around it.

The minute of grace freed her so suddenly that she wasn't conscious of starting to run. Which way? Her brain shared the release of her body; it reminded her that when she had left Yocum Farm the rain had been at her back. She faced the slanting drops, anchored the direction in her mind and took to the woods. She had run before, but never faster or more cunningly than now. At first she thought she had lost her pursuer, but apparently he had paused only to pick up her tracks. From far behind came a crash of breaking branches, and all too soon a nearer one. She took to using her head, literally; she would lower it and butt through a thicket, low down. Such chances were few and the method was tearing her shirt to shreds. But she didn't mind, because after each wriggling plunge she seemed to have gained.

Through all the Barrens, thickets spell descent. Unconsciously she was edging down toward a bottom so massed with growth it would stop a yearling bull. Her heart sank as she realized the trap she had set for herself; soon she wouldn't be able to move at all. She stood still and listened. Not a sound. For a moment she couldn't believe it; then her lips curled in a smile and she began to rest, standing up. It can be done. Her lungs, her heart and her legs were as grateful as if she had been lying flat on her back. She let minutes pass before she began to creep along between bottom and woods. Without warning, a miracle befell, discovered by her feet before she looked down. She was standing in a path, narrow and slippery with mud.

She knew she had never been on it before, but looking ahead and to the right, she caught the outline of a mighty beech. Surely there could be no second tree its equal, and she closed her eyes in order to see better. Between it and her there would be the deep black pool that had once fed the raceway bordering the far side of the tarn. Beyond gaped the broken bridge. If she followed the path on which she stood, it couldn't help but strike into the path that would lead her to the ramp. Home! How many miles had she traveled since climbing down the silver maple? Ten? Twenty? More? It didn't matter, because now she felt as fresh as when she had started—fresher! She wished she dared laugh again, louder than the last time, but guessed she'd better not.

She broke into a trot, and at the first bend the pool came into view just as she had known it would. Today it was neither still nor black; lashed by a rain, wind and flying branches, it had the angry look of boiling water. She increased her pace, and around the next turn stood the man. She couldn't stop, and drove between his braced forearms as tight as rope into clothespin. Terror froze her throat and stopped her heart, until she remembered how easily she had made a fool of Teller on the day she had brought him from school to Yocum Farm. But this was something different and unknown. She had thought she was strong; only now did she learn what strength could be. She had thought her size average; against this man's thigh she became a midget. Her jaws could crack a hickory nut, yet her teeth couldn't make a dent in the muscle jammed against her mouth. Even the toughness of her own body became a handicap, adding rage to the man's fury. Dangling her with one hand, he started slapping her head from side to side.

"Sneakin', snoopin', half-growed size o' nothin'," he grunted. "I'll larn ye to stay nigher to home!"

His hands crumpled down her arms to her waist, stripping what was left of her shirt. They kept on down her thighs until his fingers locked on her knees. His touch and the stench of him sickened her even before he swung and threw her as Rumble had been thrown. She went gyrating through the tops of the alders until her right leg cracked against the bole of a tree. Mud, almost liquid, received her softly and revived her. She seized on a hummock and dragged her head free, but when she tried to rise, she found she couldn't; her right leg wouldn't work. She kept still and listened, hoping her assailant would think she was dead, and at last she heard the crackle of twigs as footsteps hurried away.

Using her good leg as a sled to carry the other, she dug in with her elbows, propelling herself only inches at a time. When she grew tired, she would lie flat on her stomach and wonder how far it was to the junction with the main path. To reach it was her only hope, because if Nath should go to the little store after seeing Tibby, it would shame him not to cross through Oxhead Woods. Get that far and Nath would find her. The rain had lessened, but the deepening hue of the leaden sky warned her that night was about to fall. She had been gone all day. Had anybody missed her? Of course, but that didn't mean they'd worry for a minute. With the last of her strength, she dragged herself over a sharp rise into the wider path, dropped her head on a folded arm and passed out.

It wasn't for lack of time that Nath hadn't gone to the store. He had quarreled with Tibby fairly early, neither of them quite knowing how or why. Perhaps what had riled their nerves was the incessant rain, punctuated by constant gusts of wind. Perhaps it was being cooped up along with other people, even though they paid no attention to what you said or did. Then what about Yocum Farm? Had he felt cooped up there, surrounded by Pete, Lottie, Ellen, and even that nitwit Lott? Meg—in his thoughts he had left out Meg. Why? He frowned, and that was the moment when the quarrel had started.

"If it gives you such a pain being here with me," said Tibby, "why don't you go out and play boats in the gutter or run back to Meg and your old Yocum Farm?"

"I'm tired of answering that same old question," said Nath, rising, "but the general idea sounds good to me. Now sing the rest of the song. Tell me I needn't come back."

She was too stunned to answer; sick with silent anger she let him go. He caught a ride into the village and another out the County Road. Though he was in time for the late Sunday dinner, he felt ashamed to go into the house, because it would look as if he couldn't bear to lose a meal out of his wages. He climbed to his room, drowsed for a couple of hours, then came down to do his chores early and get them out of the way. Now he was entitled to supper, should there happen to be any, and after a wash, he entered the kitchen.

"Where's Meg?" asked Ellen crossly.

"How should I know?" said Nath.

"Why, ain't she been with you?" asked Ellen, the sharpness gone from her voice. "She didn't come to dinner; she was gone from her room."

Pete gave a sudden puff. "Down the silver maple as smooth as a whip snake," he muttered; "down and off through the rain."

Nath's frown matched the quick furrow on Ellen's and Lottie's foreheads. "Don't sound right for Meg to miss a meal," he said. "Ain't anybody been to look for her? Didn't anybody bother to step outside and call?"

"I did," said Lottie. "I called high and I called low."

"Anybody know what time she left?" asked Nath. Abruptly he turned to Pete. "You know. What time did she go?"

"Eleven o'clock, said Pete.

Nath stepped outside and paused under the arbor, uncertain which way to turn. Ought he to search the barn first? No; not after all the clutter of milking. A lonely whimper came from the dog-house and promptly gave his brain direction. Would he need a flashlight? What for? What good would it do in a fight? He picked up the old ax handle he had carried once before, tucked it under his arm and loosed the dog. They went down the ramp as on that other night, but the moment they entered the path, Nath felt Rumble brush by and heard the pattering of his paws, going away. He started to call him back, but thought better of it and slogged along, indifferent to branches no wetter than himself. Suddenly something leaped against his chest, scaring him stiff. It was Rumble. He squirmed, whimpered and started making short dashes down the path and back again. Nath broke into a run, and it was Rumble that saved him from trampling on Meg. He sank beside her and lifted her head.

"Meg," he whispered. "Meg!" he repeated loudly.

She woke with a sigh. "Hello, Nath. I knew you'd come."

Her head settled back as if she wanted to sleep again, but he wouldn't have it. "Meg, what happened? Are you hurt?"

"Yes," she said thoughtfully, "I am. I think I've got a broken leg."

His hand passed down over her body. "Why, your shirt's clean gone!"

"It's sort of torn," she admitted.

His hand moved gently along her right thigh, passed her knee and stopped. "It's broke all right," he said. "Now listen. Keep Rumble close by you. I'll be back as soon as I can."

"Nath!" she cried. "Don't go!"

"Why? You afraid?"

"No, no! I've got something important I got to tell you —awfully important."

"Let it wait," said Nath. He ran all the way to the house and threw open the lean-to door. "Hey, you, Pete!" he panted. "Telephone for Doc Byrne! Meg has broke her leg!"

Stopping for no chatter, he went to rout out Lot and find a plank. Together they rushed it to where Meg was waiting, and slipped it under her back. Nath fastened her legs above the break with his belt, covered her to the neck with his jacket and tied her fast with its sleeves. Thus secured, they dared lift the plank to their shoulders and made quick time to the house. The stairs presented a difficulty, narrow and with two turns, but in the excitement it occurred to nobody to take Meg anywhere save to her own room. Nath walked backward, feeling for each step. Aided by Lottie and with Ellen carrying a candle, Lot did his best to keep the plank level.

The knotted sleeves of the jacket came undone and it started to slip, but Nath could do nothing about it except to look away. Lot trampled on a sleeve and dragged the jacket clean off. The minute they let the plank down on Meg's bed, the way Ellen pushed Nath and Lot out of the room and down the stairs, you'd think they had committed some sort of crime, breaking their backs to fetch home a girl with a broken leg. Lot asked nothing better than to go back to bed, but Nath was hungry. Before he could do anything about it, the doctor's car came up the lane, honking to make sure Rumble was tied. He wasn't, and the fury of his barking lifted Pete out of his chair. He stumped into the hall, tore open the unused front door and stepped out on the porch.

"Drive right around!" he shouted.

Nath dashed past him and seized Rumble. "Come in this way, doc. Go right upstairs."

A long half hour passed before Dr. Byrne came down to report two broken ribs besides the leg. "How did it happen?" he asked.

"Nobody knows but her," said Nath; "that's the way I found her a mile from here."

"Down the silver maple as slick as a whip snake," muttered Pete.

The doctor glanced at him uneasily. After all, what did it matter how somebody broke anything? "Is that dog still loose?" he asked.

"No," said Nath. "I chained him."

He sat staring straight at Pete for some time after the doctor had gone, but Pete avoided staring back. Nath recollected how Pete was boss in his own house, and a shrewd look narrowed his eyes.

"Say," he said, "you better start searching for another helper."

That did it; Pete jounced like a shaken jelly and shot

a glance as sharp as a two-pronged fork. "Why? What's ailing you, bub?"

"I haven't ate since breakfast," said Nath. "I'm hungry."

"Ellen!" bellowed Pete. "Lottie!"

The two women hurried down from Meg's room, Ellen ahead. "What's wrong with you?" she asked testily. "Why the hollering?"

"Nath be hungry," said Pete.

"What of it?" asked Ellen, her eyes anchored grimly on the floor. "Better he should eat with Lot anyways, him and Lot!"

Pete hurled his stick clattering across the room, not at her, but close enough to give everybody a scare. "You and Lottie feed the lad durn quick," he ordered, "or ye'll be hunting somewheres else to feed yourselves."

IX

NATH couldn't make Ellen out; or Lottie, either. For days they acted as if Meg lay at the door of death instead of having only a few broken bones. He wasn't allowed to see her, and Pete couldn't climb the stairs. He asked Ellen how Meg had come to get hurt, but she said Meg didn't know or wouldn't tell. With Lottie and Ellen chasing meals up to her and staying until she ate the last bite, Nath and Pete had plenty of time to glower at each other, saying scarcely a word. Twice Nath started toward the village to see Tibby, but wondering about what Meg had wanted to tell him that was so important would get his feet to dragging until he found they had stopped of their own accord. Already it was Friday night. Would Tibby come out as usual on Sunday? Had anybody told her what had happened?

He headed for town, but short of the lane he slowed like a car out of gas and came to a stop. Presently he turned and went back. The moon, just past its full, bulged into view ahead and emphasized the outline of the main house. It was completely dark, and no glimmer showed from the plank cabin, either; but as he started toward the wagon shed he caught a blur of light against the foliage of the big maple. It drew him down to the icehouse to stare upward at Meg's open window. He didn't dare call, for fear of waking Ellen or Pete, but he simply had to talk to Meg. He began to climb, hoping she would guess who it was before she got scared. He knew better than to follow out along the branch nearest the window; instead he chose a higher one and let his weight bring it so close that a frond swished inside the room. He laid one hand on the sill and steadied himself, listening.

"It's Nath," he murmured.

"I know," breathed Meg; "I've been watching you against the moonlight. Come inside or they'll hear us."

He got one leg over the sill, cautiously jammed the branch under a shutter, and a moment later was kneeling beside the bed. The moon filled the room with a shimmer of light. Within the blot of her hair, black against the pillow, Meg's face became a white blur, but out of it shone two eyes bright enough for headlights, so bright he could see them talk and almost hear them laugh.

"Oh, Nath," she whispered, "I'm awful glad you've come. Why did you wait so long?"

"Just dumb, I guess," whispered Nath. "I wasn't let up

the stairs and never thought of the tree until tonight. How are you? Does it hurt a lot?"

"Oh, that!" exclaimed Meg impatiently. "That part don't worry me." They had been unconscious of holding hands, but now she pressed his, hard. "Nath, listen. I've—I've found the Red House." His fingers closed on hers tighter and tighter while she told him exactly what had happened. "That man!" she gasped at the end. "I never saw him before. I didn't know there could be anybody like that."

"Reds Truman," muttered Nath, his palms wet with the sweat of anger. "He's Teller's father, and so tough his hide would turn buckshot."

"Oh," said Meg, her mind snapping back to Teller's warning to stay out of Oxhead Woods. "Say, Nath, I haven't seen Teller for an awful long while."

"Nobody has. I guess he smelled the draft coming and he's gone."

"Where?"

"Ask the mushies or any other kind of rat—or best, a skunk. If Teller was amind to, he could stay in the woods and marshes for years without anybody laying an eye on him, and come out fatter than he went in."

They heard a rumble from downstairs, Pete talking in his sleep—or was he asleep? They scarcely breathed, waiting to find out which.

Meg reached to pull Nath's head close to hers. "Better go," she whispered, "but come back tomorrow—every day."

Her hair tickled his nose, and he had to rub it against her neck to keep from sneezing. That made her want to laugh, and the only way to stop it was to press her mouth hard against his face. It was so like a kiss, he answered it without thinking, pressing his lips to her soft cheek. They drew apart, startled and abruptly sobered. He left her, crept to the window, and presently was sliding off the ice-house to the ground. But all night long he was restless, and every time he woke he wondered if Pete had heard. Even after breakfast, because looking at Pete was like waiting for a boulder to talk, he kept on wondering. You couldn't guess Pete going or coming, except to remember he was sure boss in his own house. Take the way he had bawled out Ellen and Lottie, ordering them to fetch food. They'd done it, hadn't they? Nath frowned.

"Say, Pete," he said loudly, "I want to see Meg. Okay for me to go up?"

"Sure, sure," said Pete. After a slight puff, he added, "But use the stairs."

Nath colored so violently that he thought Ellen would notice, but she was looking angrily at Pete. "He'll not," she said emphatically. "He's no boy, he's a man, and men don't go traipsing into girls' bedrooms, not in this house!"

"What call to," asked Pete, a malevolent gleam in his eye, "when all they need do is wait till the gals come knocking on their door? . . . Go ahead up, Nath. Find out what happened."

Ellen followed Nath and entered Meg's room close behind him. "Nath!" cried Meg. "It's been days and days! Why wouldn't you come to see me?"

"I wasn't let," said Nath. "Seem's you can go swimming with girls in next to nothing, but if you see them with a broken leg, it's somehow going against two dozen commandments I never heard of."

"There's only one commandment," said Ellen sharply, "and it holds all the rest. Live decent."

Meg studied her gravely. What if she should blurt right

out where she'd been? Could this Ellen still blush? Would it be fun to see? No, no; you couldn't make a joke of it, even Pete couldn't. What if that other girl was still here, listening inside Ellen? What if she should step out and tears gush from her eyes like pouring rain? How would you feel? What would there be left to say? Would she ever forgive you or you forgive yourself?

"That's right," said Meg, "and I can't think what you're both fussing about. All I know, if it wasn't for Nath, I'd be dead."

"How did it happen, anyways?" asked Nath. His eyes had a wicked twinkle, as if it amused him to put it up to her to spin a plausible tale from scratch. "Pete wants to know."

Meg shot scorn at him and drew a long breath. "Remember the big poplar," she recited earnestly, "the one with the patch of mistletoe where you said no man could climb to it, let alone a girl? I guess I wanted to show you, even if I broke my neck. I pushed up between the trunk and a mat of greenbrier thick enough for a ladder. I'd kick my heels into it, shut my eyes and push. The more the briers tore my shirt the madder I got, but it worked and I got up into the branches. That mistletoe is awful high, and the way it was raining turned the back of the tree to grease. All of me slipped all at once. That's how."

Nath gawked at her in admiration, but Ellen merely shrugged. "Huh," she sniffed, "what's so secret about that? Why couldn't you of told instead of making a mystery until now?"

"Only Nath has seen the mistletoe," explained Meg sweetly, "and without knowing just how it is, nobody'd possibly believe you could break a leg and two ribs."

"Besides losing your shirt," murmured Nath.

The next morning he hung around nervously, wondering if Tibby would come. Though she had started early, dressed in her snappiest play suit, he was in for a long wait. The easiest way for her would have been to bike out the County Road, but she had been in no hurry and had chosen to walk, following the route she had taken with Meg and Nath the first time she went to Yocum Farm. The start was easy, but deep in the woods she came to a fork she couldn't remember. Everything was changed, for after an unusually cold spring an incredible lushness had come to every bush and tree. Whichever way she chose, she would have to push through crowding foliage, but since Yocum Farm must be somewhere off to the left, that was the fork she took. Presently the trees grew larger and the undergrowth all but disappeared. She was sure she had never seen this glade before, but it was so lovely that she dawdled on, swinging the big straw hat she always carried on hot sunny days.

A frown that had nothing to do with losing the way wrinkled her forehead, and trouble clouded her eyes. Ever since she could remember, for ages, other girls had conceded she was first best, Meg Yarrow along with the rest. They still did, Meg included, but what about Nath Storm? She couldn't make him out. Though she had watched him with Meg day after day, never once had she surprised a single glance that threatened her own supremacy. Yet she sensed he was edging away from her and that it was high time she taught him a lesson. Why was he so pig-set on working at Yocum Farm? Why couldn't he be helping her father instead? Today was when she was going to find out, once and for all.

She threw up her head, and her eyes met two other eyes. She wasn't one to be frightened by anybody she knew, and she wasn't frightened now.

"Hello, Teller."

"Hello," he answered. He was standing hooked to the low limb of a tree by one arm with his ankles crossed, and he had been watching her for some time. "Lost, ain't ye?"

"Not specially," said Tibby. "I'm not in a hurry to get anywheres."

"Heading for Yocum's?"

"Yes, I guess so."

"That's why I waited. I could of cleared off and you wouldn't never of seen me."

"Sure, you could. But why would you? Scared of having somebody just lay eyes on you?"

"You said it," answered Teller with a scowl. "I wouldn't let anybody see me but you, Tibby, because I figure you're the kind has more sense in her head as ever comes out through her mouth."

"I'm tired," said Tibby, seating herself on the flat root of the tree.

He took it as an invitation and slid down to sit half facing her.

"You got looks and all the rest besides, but that ain't why I waited. I wanted to warn ye to lay off Yocum's and the woods beyond. They ain't healthy. Look what happened to Meg."

"When?" asked Tibby, startled. "What?"

Teller smiled. "So Nath ain't bothered to tell ye! Somebody caught her in Oxhead Woods one week gone and busted her up for fair. She ain't been out since."

"You? Was it you, Teller?"

"Heck, no. If it was me, would I be risking my hide to warn ye off?"

"That's silly. You aren't risking a thing."

"Say, Tibby, you trying to play dumb? This war won't last forever, and if I don't hear of it until it's over, where's the harm?"

"Oh," said Tibby, catching her breath. "You could be working," she added quickly. "It's people that work that help the people that go."

He grinned at her. "What about them as buys bonds? Don't they help?" He dragged out a roll and began peeling off bills. "Do me a favor?"

"What?" she asked, stricken by the sight of so much money.

"First time you're up to Philly buy me half a dozen fifty-dollar bonds. Here's enough cash and ten extra for your trouble."

"Oh, I couldn't!"

He seized her arm and thrust the notes deep inside her blouse. She thought she was in for a fight, but before she could move, much less speak, he was on his feet and away from her. "Sure you can," he said, as smooth as butter, "and keep your mouth shut, to boot. Bring 'em here any Sunday morning, and by that time happen I'll want some more. Didn't you say it was up to me to help? What about you? If you haven't got the grit to do your share, just quit picking on me or anybody else."

"Why couldn't I buy them in Salem?" she asked, weakening.

"Aw, use your bean," said Teller disgustedly. "Want everybody hounding to know where Tibby Rinton got the money? Up to Philly nobody would care."

"Just this once," she decided finally. She fished out the bills, divided them and packed them methodically into her shoes, flat as an inner sole. "There!"

"My, my!" chuckled Teller. "Only a sharp one would of thought of that!"

She rose. "I guess I better go now."

"This way," said Teller. "It'll save all of a mile."

They descended to the sharp bank of a run. Indifferent to wetting his trousers, he stepped into the muddy water, and when he turned, his shoulders were on a level with her thighs. He locked one arm around her legs above the knees and lifted her so easily that she might have been standing on a platform. His strength and the touch of his bare arm on her flesh combined to send such a thrill through her that she was breathing harder than he when he set her down on the far side.

"There you are," he said. "Follow straight through till you hit a path, then turn right. Afore you know it, you'll break into the lane."

"Thanks," she murmured, lifting her eyes to his face. "Thanks a lot."

He caught her elbows lightly and laughed down at her. "Yeah? Then what about paying?"

"How much?" she asked.

"Only one—like this!"

She had been kissed often before, and by more than one boy, but Teller's kiss was different. Though it hadn't lasted long, it followed her like a whip, driving her so fast along the trail that she stumbled more than once.

X

NATH saw Tibby hurrying up the lane and went to meet her. She was out of breath and stared at him as if she faced a stranger; it wasn't that he was different from himself, but so different from Teller. It shocked her into wondering what she'd better say. Either she had to tell him everything or pretend she hadn't heard about Meg, pretend like mad about the rest too. Never had her beauty flamed more violently. Her pale cheeks were bright and her lips alive with color, but strangest of all was a sort of swirl in her eyes that made them seem as breathless as the rest of her. Nath felt flattered by her haste and then uneasy.

"Why all the rush so late?" he asked.

"Whose fault if I'm late?" she said sharply. "Yours—that's who. You've been so queer lately I couldn't make up my mind. I was ready early. I had my bike out, then I put it back. Finally, I just sort of started for a walk and got lost. What's the matter with you, anyway? You're a fine one to be picking on me! Where've you been all week?"

Nath frowned. "Haven't you heard about Meg?"

"No! What?"

"She fell out of a tree last Sunday and broke two ribs and a leg, but she's getting well fast."

"My goodness! Fell out of a tree? How on earth?" Tibby could feel her color deepening from the way she was lying. "Say," she continued angrily, "why couldn't you come in and tell me, all this time?"

"I been mighty busy, Tibby," said Nath conciliatingly. "Anyways, I sort of thought you'd hear it from the doc.

Why don't you go ahead up and let Meg give you all the dope?"

"All right," said Tibby, looking hard at him, "but afterwards you and me had better have a talk."

Because she saw that Pete was drowsing, Tibby passed through the kitchen with only a murmured word, and presently was listening to Meg spin her tale about climbing for the mistletoe. It gave her a kick to make her tell it twice, knowing all the time that she was lying from start to finish. But why? What reason was there to lie? What had really happened? Meg looked prettier than ever before in her life. The glow of convalescence was in her cheeks and the shine of it in her eyes. Had Nath been seeing her this way? Of course he had. Tibby didn't have to fake interest in the tale. With lips parted and eyes wide, she wished she dared lean over, take Meg by the throat and choke the truth out of her.

"My," she said, "I'd like to see how high is that mistletoe. When you going to get up?"

"I don't know," said Meg. "I feel fine. Bet I could do it now, soon as I get some crutches. Nath's making a pair. He says he can make 'em as good as bought."

Tibby rose. "I wouldn't think he'd have time, the way he says he's been so busy. I'll come see you soon again, Meg."

She went downstairs, looking for Nath. Dinner was ready to serve, with Ellen fussing over the table and Lottie near the range. Pete half woke from his doze, and his eyes happened to open mistily on Tibby.

"Elspeth," he murmured so softly Tibby alone could hear. "Here at last." She paused before him, puzzled. "Lass, I been honing for your coming, to tell ye once more and ever again how close I hold ye in my love. My hand is a cup and you the cool spring water, answer to a lad's thirst and every question of the heart. I love your fair beauty and all your ways. Just the sight of you is food for the soul, feeding the roots of eternal life."

Tibby took him for crazy, so crazy it wasn't even funny. Was he looking at her or wasn't he? She couldn't be sure. Anyways, hadn't he seen her enough times not to mix her with somebody that was dead and gone? Now he was reaching out a pudgy hand. Should she take it? Why not? His fingers closed over hers and tightened slowly. She stifled a gasp. His hand wasn't soft at all; it had the strength of a vise. Though it stopped short of hurting her, she knew she could no more draw away than pull down a mountain. She stared at his face in wonder and fright. His eyes were pools of mist, and little drops of sweat began to pop out on his forehead.

"Hell hold ye for aye, Hube Snell," he muttered. "Did ye think with one loud cry to drown out the anguished screams of years?"

"Let me go," said Tibby huskily. "Please, please!"

At the sound of her voice, his head jerked upward and he came wide awake so quickly that it gave her another shock. "Howdy," he said in his natural tone. "Seems you're just in time for dinner."

As he started hunching his chair toward the head of the table, Nath came in. Looking around gave him a feeling that something was lacking. "What about bringing Meg down?" he asked. "I could do it easy as carrying a bucket."

"You set," said Ellen. "Meg will eat where she lies."

"Why so?" asked Pete. "I ain't seen the gal since her trouble, and Nath's idea sounds real good. . . . Fetch her, Nath."

"No," protested Ellen. "He might drop her, and all would be to do over again."

Pete's fist crashed on the table so hard that a blob of the creamy mashed potatoes rose up in a ludicrous peak. "Fetch her!"

Nath wished he had kept his mouth shut, and looked miserably at Tibby. "Come on, Tib; give us a hand."

"What for?" she asked icily. "Two hands to one bucket?"

"Wait," said Ellen to Nath. She hurried upstairs, and in a matter of minutes Meg was clothed in a fresh white nightie with a tucked square yoke and flounce at the wrists long enough to flare like snowy tulips from the sleeves of her dressing gown. Her cheeks glowed with excitement and she started bouncing her hips up and down.

"Stop that!" said Ellen gently. "Want to spoil things before you get started?" She added, scarcely raising her voice, "You can come in now."

Nath lifted Meg carefully. Her ribs were thickly taped and the cast on her leg threw her out of balance, but he adjusted his hold accordingly. She sat in his arms with her legs straight out. At first he thought it was going to be easy, a game they had played before. But who had handed him a baby to hold this time? Himself. Presently he frowned. Meg wasn't helping. She was making herself heavy the way anybody can, heavy as lead. Slowly she jack-knifed at the hips and began to sag. He could feel laughter gurgling inside her; she was doing it on purpose. In a minute he would have to let her down on the stairs in front of everybody.

"Quit it," he whispered, "or I'll bite your ear, same as they do a mule. Want I should bite?"

She knew he meant it, and threw one arm around his

neck, helping him. He eased her into two chairs on Pete's right. Tibby sat opposite her and Nath took the next seat. The food was so good that it blotted out thought as well as talk. Even after the table was cleared, the way Pete, the two girls and Nath had stuffed held them inside a sort of somnolence from which Lottie and Ellen were excluded. Busy with the dishes, they seemed banished to a separate world. Pete gave his shoulders a shake, gripped the arms of his chair and leaned forward, staring straight ahead.

"Did ye find it?" he murmured.

Only Meg realized to whom he was speaking. "Yes," she whispered.

Pete sucked in a sigh, a sound as thin as the scurrying of a mouse into a haystack. "Yep," he chirped, still not looking at anybody, "reckon you seen it, true enough. And what did you pay? Two broke ribs and a busted leg. Happen that's all, ye got off cheap."

"It was all," said Meg, "and twice more than enough."

"Women pays one way," said Pete, "men another. Lucky it wa'n't Nath seen the house."

Nath glanced at Tibby's profile, lower lip hanging in the blank expression of one completely at a loss. Half of him wanted to laugh, but the other half itched to play with fire. "I saw it, too, Pete. Three weeks ago, and I haven't yet begun to swell."

"Give it time," muttered Pete. His head made a quarter-turn and his eyes wrapped themselves around Tibby, holding her so tight it made it hard for her to breathe. "You too?" he asked. "Did you look upon it?"

"What are you all talking about?" stammered Tibby. "I think you're crazy. Look on what?"

"The Red House," said Pete.

"That!" exclaimed Tibby. "All this fuss about a rotten little old house that—that——"

"Sure she saw it," said Nath, "same as me. But we never could find it again; only Meg."

Pete settled back and gave a puff. "No road dies," he said. "Folks die, but never a road. Pines can spring up in one of them ancient trails thick as wheat, but the trace remains. A hundred roads leads to the Red House, all on 'em alive. Life follers 'em in, only death comes back."

"I'm not dead, Uncle Pete," said Meg softly.

"So?" said Pete loudly. "What of Elspeth? What about Ellen? Ain't Ellen dead? There she stands. Ask her."

Ellen pretended not to hear; she was wiping plates two at a time and letting them down with a clatter. Lottie dried her hands, turned and came marching across the room, straight and strong as a totem pole. Her nose was like a prow and her blue eyes had taken on a sort of concentrated heat. She gripped the back of Pete's chair, whirled it around and pushed it rumbling across the floor until his feet dangled inside the fireplace.

"Sit there," she whispered. "One more word out of you and I'll sink the poker in your neck."

Meg stared unbelievingly. Tibby sprang up and hurried toward the door. Nath followed her through the lean-to and out into the grape arbor. She whirled on him, panting.

"What's the matter with the people in there? Are they batty? And you! I've had enough of them and you too. I'm through. From now on, you can go any road you like and I'll go mine. Good-by to nothing!" He laid his hand on her arm, but she shook it off. "I mean it. I'm tired of Mr. Lordawmighty Nash Storm treating me like—like middlings and hogwash."

Anger had brought her to life in a blooming so sudden that it had the violence of a flood. He was shaken. All the threads that had been holding them to Yocum's Farm—little things such as amusement over Pete's looks and maunderings, curiosity, his own good-natured humoring of Meg's fears—snapped and turned him adrift. Hadn't Tibby been his anchor for years? Why was he chucking it away? For what? Does any girl like to be traded in against nothing? No wonder she was sore. He took her by the elbows and forced her to look at him.

"Name what you want I should do, Tib," he said, "and I'll do it."

Her breath seemed to catch and hang poised before she answered. "Honest?"

"Sure," said Nath. "Anything you ask."

She was in his arms before he knew it, her face raised to his. "Oh, Nath, you know what I want. Get out of here. Leave today. Then you and me can be like we used to be."

"All right," he agreed, but the two short words had the drag of a lengthening shadow.

It drew his thoughts away from the girl in his arms, not pointing at Meg or any other individual, just marking a dark path that ended in a question without an answer. Absently, his hand smoothed Tibby's back, and though its pressure lacked insistence, she yielded to its touch with a suddenness that jolted him wide awake. A flame seemed to leap in her, reaching, searching for something it didn't find. To his amazement, there was a door between them a door that wouldn't open. He tugged at it furiously, angry only at himself.

"We'll get married, Tibby," he said hoarsely, "as soon as ever you want."

To add to his bewilderment, she cooled and drew back. With her hands against his chest, her eyes traveled mockingly across his troubled face. "It's about time you came to your senses," she said with a short laugh, "high time. Go get your things."

He frowned. Though this was a familiar Tibby he thought he could handle, he was gripped by regret for the stranger so swiftly come and gone.

"Now?" he asked coolly.

"Now or never. You can go to our place or over to the store."

"But what about Meg?"

"Meg?" said Tibby sharply. "Well, what about her?"

"Who's to carry her back to bed?"

"With that woman Lottie around?" jeered Tibby. "She could carry her with one hand."

"I got to tell them, haven't I?" said Nath, flushing. "You wait here."

When he went inside, Pete hadn't moved and Lottie had gone back to help Ellen finish the dishes. Nath crossed straight to Meg. Without saying anything, he raised her, carried her upstairs and braced her against the pillows. Looking down at her, the promise he had made to Tibby suddenly became absurdly enlarged into a cowardly betrayal, and he could feel his heart squeezing into a knot the way it does when you have to drown a litter of puppies.

"Meg," he gulped, "I'm awful sorry, but I got to get out of here."

She laughed up at him. "Sure you have!"

"I mean over to my place, over to the store," he explained unsmilingly.

A shadow struck across her eyes, giving them the depth

of the tarn. They measured him slowly, as if to fix forever his image in her mind. This wasn't the white-fleshed boy of that first day at the pump or even the tanned body, with a welt across the back, of their first swim. The way a sapling grows out of itself into a tree, Nath had evolved into a stalwart trunk against which she had learned to lean. Now he was going away, out of reach.

"You're leaving," she said, her eyes staring beyond him; "going away for good."

"Yeah, that's about the size of it."

She threw out her hand, and when he took it, he could feel her listening to the distant rumble of her ancient fears, advancing like a stampeding herd. But it was his fingers that began to tremble, and abruptly hers closed on them in a steadfast grip. She drew him down and their eyes mingled in a long question that, like the lengthening shadow, had no answer. Their lips barely touched. Hers, warm and tender, held an incredible innocence that seemed to translate his spirit into a quivering wing above a flower. Was this a kiss or what? Confusion shook him. Meg wasn't playing fair. She had a right to stay what she'd always been, somebody as comfortable as an old shoe. Now she was butting into none of her business, tangling him with more than the shame he already felt at turning his back on the Yocum Farm. Her whisper came to him from a long way off, "Good-by, Nath."

XI

EXASPERATION merged into a feeling of defeat as Nath started downstairs; whichever way he turned he could consider himself licked—no good to Meg, Tibby or himself. He stopped on the last step to take farewell of the kitchen. No longer did it seem divided into separate counties. It had become one, a compact world from which his own act was about to banish him. All the questions that had troubled Meg would trouble him no more, except the great question of himself. He scowled. How could a farm—a place you'd never even seen three months ago—make you or break you? Perhaps it couldn't. Perhaps he was just dreaming things. He crossed over to face Pete.

"Mr. Yocum," he said, "I'm leaving."

Pete shook himself awake. "Eh? How's that? Who's Mr. Yocum? Huh! Me?" Abruptly, his eyes blazed. "Leaving? What do you mean, leaving?"

"I'll do your chores tonight," said Nath, "but beginning tomorrow you'll have to get along with Lot."

"Ah," breathed Pete. "I git ye. Skeered. Skeered to stay and learn the rest of it. Busting your gut and mine to git clear o' the Red House. Hark to my judgment on ye. Men stands up, but God created also the yellow-bellied worm."

"Worm yourself!" said Nath hotly. "D'you think I'm afraid of you or the drivel of your fancy tales? Muck. That's the name for them, and you too."

"Think so, eh?" whispered Pete hoarsely. "Oh, no, ye don't! The grip of that muck is on ye. It'll never let go, and who knows it best? You, liar as well as worm."

Nath turned white, but when he spoke it was quietly, giving care to each word. "Perhaps you're right. Perhaps I'm a coward in some ways and a liar at times. But here's the truth, Pete. You're the hog grown fat to busting on your own young. Who's the worst coward, you or me? Would you dare pick on Lottie? The hell you would! Only on a kid since she was five years old, scaring her night and day with your filthy lies."

A slap stung his cheek, the sting of it piercing to the bone. Lottie? Had Lottie hit him? No—Ellen. He couldn't believe it. Tears sprang to his eyes, not from the hurt, but because it was Ellen who had struck him. Through a mist, he saw Pete start to rise, then sit again, knowing full well that on his toddling feet a push from anybody's finger could send him rolling. Instead, he hunched his chair forward with a violence that made it hump like a rabbit. The glare of his eyes lit up the purple in his cheeks and a croaking was coming out of him, puffing the hair away from his mouth. Short words, each word a club, "Hold him! His throat! One hand! Only one!"

Ellen swung into his path, close against Nath. She slipped an arm around him and with her other hand stroked the cheek she had slapped. Her fingers had a tenderness so like to Meg's kiss that Nath felt another surge of confusion, as if Ellen could turn herself into the twin of Meg.

"Dear Nath," she whispered, "I'm sorry, so sorry! Please go. Quick, Nath. Please!"

"Hurry!" shouted Lottie.

Her cry, sharp as a goad, drove Nath toward the lean-to door just as Pete drew near enough to seize on Ellen. His hand gave only a childish flip, yet it sent her reeling across the room, and she would have spun clean to the wall if the heavy table hadn't saved her.

"Nath!" screamed Meg's voice from upstairs. "Ellen! Nath!"

"It's all right, Meg!" called Ellen in a clear voice. "I'm coming!"

"Get out, you, Nath!" screamed Lottie. "Git!"

Nath hesitated, but only for an instant. What would be the use of turning back? Could he hit an old man sitting in a chair? Yet when he got outside, he was panting as if he had run a long way. His senses as well as his eyes were blurred, and when Tibby came up to him, her face gay with laughter, she seemed an apparition, a reminder of a forgotten world. What business had she here? None. As for that, what of himself? Wasn't he an outsider too? An echo jeered at him: *The grip is on ye; it'll never let go.*

"Well, you did it!" chortled Tibby. "I didn't get it all, but I heard plenty. You did it right, Nath!" He brushed her aside. She froze, color ebbing swiftly from her face. "I should think you'd be glad. Why, you ought to get down on your knees and thank me, instead of pushing me around."

"Perhaps I ought," said Nath in a lifeless tone. "A guy thinks he can wander anywhere in the world, take any road he pleases. Then he wakes to a hog-tight fence on his left and another on his right. How many ways to go does that leave him? You tell me."

Tibby stared at him blankly, baffled by an unknown language. "Just as you say, Nath; only let's get out of here."

"Not till I've done the chores."

"You think I'm going to wait around all that time?"

"You don't have to."

"Where you going afterwards? Over to our place?"

"Not today," said Nath. "Guess I'll go back to the store."

"You're spoiling everything," exploded Tibby; "just everything!"

Nath looked her full in the eyes, misery in his own. "Tib," he said dully, "I've tried to play fair with you and everybody else. The only one I've double-crossed going and coming is me." He turned toward the plank cabin and raised his voice. "Hey, Lot!"

Lot appeared in the open doorway. "What you want?"

"Get in the cows for me, will you?"

Lot squinted at the sun. " 'Tain't time."

"You get 'em in fast," said Nath, "or you'll do the milking by your lonesome. Today and tomorrow too."

He looked around, but Tibby was gone. He watched her disappear down the lane, then climbed into his room to pack, and by the time he was ready the cows were stabled. He and Lot finished the chores, then Nath fetched out a pair of crutches.

"All these need is a bit more rubbing," he said. "You rub 'em down good, Lot, and soon as Meg wants 'em, Lottie can show her how they work." He picked up his bag. "Mind you don't forget now."

"You leaving?" asked Lot, his jaw sagging disconsolately.

"Yeah," said Nath absently.

"What about them six bucks?" asked Lot.

"Six bucks!" muttered Nath with a puzzled frown. "I don't know what you're talking about."

While he was hesitating which way to go with the heavy bag, Lottie called that his mother had telephoned she was on her way to the store. That settled it; he hurried straight across Oxhead Woods. He found his mother a lot thinner, yet somehow more alive. She, in turn, was struck by his sudden maturity; in the short time she had been away, he had stepped across the line between boy and man. It gave her a shy feeling, and when he put his arms around her, she kissed only his cheek.

"Seems we got to get acquainted again," he said with a smile.

"Go on!" she laughed. "I guess it's just that you're so big I felt I ought to be careful. You get that way over to the plant."

They sat down. "How's things going?" asked Nath.

"Fine. Hard work, but good pay. You don't get much time to yourself; only Sundays, and sometimes not even that. I grabbed a chance to come over today because I've got something to tell you. You're pretty well fixed, aren't you, Nath? Sort of settled?"

"Sort of," he admitted with a frown, "but not the way you think. I'm going to marry Tibby Rinton."

"Oh? That's nice. But what a look! Something wrong, son? You worried about the war?"

"Shucks, no," said Nath. "Soon as they want me, I'll go; perhaps sooner." His frown tightened. "Yeah, that might be the right idea."

"Well, no call for you to rush it, not while you're farming. Folks can't fight or work without they eat. Now let's talk about me. I'm getting married myself, Nath."

"You?" he exclaimed, flashing an astounded look to her face.

"Come, now," she laughed, "I'm not as old as all that! Thirty-four, that's how old."

He flushed and turned his eyes away. Somehow it had never entered his head that she would marry again, and the thought of it made her into somebody entirely new, sudden as lopping off a branch with an ax. The trunk of the tree was your mother, fixed and rooted; now here was the branch, free for some stranger to carry away. But why be a pig? Hadn't he been planning to leave her without giving her feelings a single thought?

"Great!" he said. "Who's the lucky guy?"

"A foreman at the plant, name of Fred Gant. You'll like him. You got to come to the wedding, Nath. Next Sunday. We won't have time to go anywheres, not even overnight."

"I'll try," said Nath. "Say, Mom, I'm quitting over at Yocum's, and I'd hate to walk in on the Rintons with hardly a cent to my name. All right for me to stay here while I save up some wages?"

"I'll do better than that, Nath. I'll sign the place over to you tomorrow and you can count it for your wedding present."

His whole face brightened, turning him into a boy again. "Gee, Mom, that's fine!"

At dawn next morning he went to work for Mr. Rinton, and from the start was too busy to give a thought to how desperately he was needed at Yocum Farm. Everybody there missed him, including the horses and cows, but Lot was the chief victim. Meg on crutches and Pete lugging his stool would follow him around from dawn to dark, telling him just what to do and then watching his addled brain not do it. Pete squealed like a roped pig and finally was driven to trying to help with more than words. Hadn't he once held the county record for stripping a heavy udder? He braced his stool just so and, tipping it forward, settled his brow against the flank of the gentlest Yocum cow. He reached and reached, but couldn't make it by a foot, and when the stool flew from under him, Meg laughed until she gasped—her first laugh since Nath's departure. Pete seized the cow's tail and hauled himself to his feet.

"You!" he sputtered, turning on Meg. "If it wa'n't your caperings through the woods had druv Nath off, all our troubles would of passed us by."

"Me?" cried Meg, quickly sobered. "Was it me called

him names? Who did the scaring? Who told fool tales, thinking to hold him here?"

"Fool tales, eh?" muttered Pete. "Huh! 'Twas the ha'nt of Hube Snell, busting your leg and all, scairt Nath so proper he run with his tail glued to his belly. No grit to him. Wormy."

"It's a lie," whispered Meg, white with fury.

Lot looked up from finishing his sixth cow. "That Nath boy bound to come back," he announced soothingly. "Soon's ever I git time to do his bidding, he'll sure come back to pay me."

Pete didn't listen, but Meg said wonderingly, "Pay you? What for?" Lot gave her a knowing look, scratched his head, nodded toward Pete and mouthed at her silently. "Dumb," she said disgustedly. "Now you can't even talk!"

One day dragged into another, each evening leaving urgent tasks undone. The doctor removed Meg's cast and untaped her ribs, warning her to be careful. Lottie took pity on her son. In a pair of his overalls she was as good as any man, and set out to get in the hay. By that time Meg could help to the extent of driving the wagon, and perched between the big fat horses and a towering load she had the look of an earnest gnome. Back at the barn, neither she nor Lottie knew anything about handling a grappling fork, and that's where Pete came in, shouting directions and managing Blackie at the end of the long track rope. Inside the house, Ellen undertook to do all the work. The farm would fall far short of its usual productiveness, but at least its inmates were getting by.

As for Nath, he also was living a scrappy existence in more senses than one. Fantastic wages were being paid for farm labor by the hour, but he was working for Mr. Rinton from dawn to dark at two dollars a day and board. Though he had breakfast and dinner with the Rintons, he seldom stayed for supper, more eager to get home for a bath than to eat. Tibby felt cheated. She had looked forward to quiet moments with him, but hadn't counted on the dead silence of exhaustion. On the first Sunday, she sulked and let him go alone to the wedding in Wilmington. On the second, she had planned a whole day together at his place, a sort of domestic picnic, but it had rained so hard she stayed at home. Had he come over? No, he hadn't bothered; all he'd done was grab the chance to sleep around the clock.

He wasn't the only cloud in her firmament. Everybody who was doing overtime, her father included, added his bit to a sodden sky. The war seemed to have set up a wall. Beyond it, half the world was up to its ears in work; this side of it, you were lonely. Suddenly her cheeks flushed, for out of nowhere the memory of Teller Truman had stung her with the flick of a lash. Was Teller worn to a rag? No; somehow he was managing to back the war effort with bonds and still stay gay. With a shock she remembered the money hidden in her room, and felt guilty. Just forgetting it was bad enough; not to have done her share in carrying out Teller's patriotic impulse was worse. It was easy to trump up an excuse to go to Philly on the bus, and still easier to buy the bonds.

With the errand done, her mind ought to have been at ease, but it wasn't. Ordinarily placid, it became a field where a game was being played with moves so intricate that she couldn't follow them. Every time she tried to think about Nath, she ended up by looking into Teller's mocking eyes. Whose fault was it? Nath's. She struck a secret bargain; she would give Nath Storm just three days to come to life. Until church time. When Sunday came, as she fussed around upstairs waiting for her father and mother to go, a fever drove her from one window to another, watching for Nath. A pier glass beckoned, and she paused before it, appraising her beauty as if it belonged to somebody else. Had it slipped? Could that be the answer to everything?

The face in the glass, flowering out of her white cotton frock, broke into a smile that made her blood leap. Now she longed for the departure of the car. Would it never go? It did at last and, snatching up the bonds, she rushed downstairs, Nath completely forgotten. She hurried across the barnyard, along the orchard and into the woods. In the sunlight, her white dress had flickered like a butterfly above the twinkle of her bobby socks, but once inside the somber woods, she slowed down and became a candle. Entering the open glade of so many Sundays ago, she wondered what she would do if Teller hadn't come. Then she saw him crouching low with his head between his knees. He didn't need to look up; he could see with his ears.

"Made up your mind to come across at last," he muttered.

She tugged the bonds from inside her bodice. "Here they are, Teller."

He rose slowly, snatched the bonds and rammed them into his hip pocket. From the waist up, his naked torso was burned as brown as a dried leaf, and his tawny hair, bleached in streaks, crept in fuzzy tendrils down his cheeks and around his neck. His eyes were more than bloodshot, red and unseeing as garnets, and the smell of him was the smell of the woods, strongly laced with the odor of liquor.

"What the heck you mean," he snarled, "standing me up? Who you think you are, anyway?"

"Why, you're drunk!" cried Tibby, catching her breath. "I'm sorry I came at all, sorry I ever bothered to get your old bonds."

As she turned to leave, he caught her by the shoulder and spun her into his arms. "I'll show you how drunk I am!"

Held too close to strike out or even kick, all she could do was to writhe with the fury of a trapped rat. His grimy hands mauled her body, and his mouth was twice as greedy. Two kinds of fire swept through her—revulsion merging into a mounting flame. Abruptly fear of herself blotted out fear of Teller, and for a second left her paralyzed. Confused by her sudden yielding, he relaxed his hold, and instantly she gave him a push so violent that he tripped on a root, went over backward and hit the ground with a bone-shaking jolt. No longer afraid, she stood looking down at him with a jeering smile. He rolled to his feet as smooth as a cat, and laughed. Her dress was a sight, smudged wherever it wasn't torn. He liked her this way, real, neighbor to dirt and himself.

"Drunk," she repeated with distaste. "You smell."

He grinned at her. "Kidding yourself, ain't ye? Hark to this, Tib. You can fool around with pretty-boy Nath much as you like, but whenever you itch for a man, it's to me your feet will bring ye."

Black loam slammed against his face and spattered in his mouth. The clod had come from over Tibby's shoulder, and before she could turn, Teller was on the run to meet Nath. They collided with a shock that bumped them apart, giving their fists a chance. Tibby stood with her jaw hanging, listening to a sound she had never heard before. It came again and again, the peculiar impact of bare knuckles reaching through flesh to bone. It sickened her, but she could neither move nor keep her eyes from watching. They saw splotches of color leap into being, and then the gush of blood. As it flowed down Teller's bare chest and stained Nath's open shirt, she grew aware of a different sort of battle inside her own mind. Whom did she want to win? Didn't she know? There wasn't a doubt as to which it would be. Teller of course. But did she want him to? He was rawhide, but Nath was rock that could crouch and shift like crazy, dodging its own inevitable crash. He was crouching now, low down, but this time, when he came up, the whole of him followed the line of his fist. It didn't seem to hit hard, and her own brain reeled with amazement as Teller's body arched over backward and fell in a crumpled heap that twitched and then lay still.

She rushed to drop on one knee beside him, and out of her eyes a stranger glared at Nath. "Had to catch him drunk!" she blazed. "Try it sometime he's sober! Just once! Try it!"

Bewilderment spread across Nath's battered face. He couldn't believe what his ears had heard or what his eyes were seeing. Teller stirred and slowly roused. His arm crooked weakly around Tibby's neck, gained strength and drew her down until their lips met in an oblivious kiss.

They hadn't forgotten Nath; they simply didn't know he was there. Anger started to grip him, but promptly loosened its hold. This was funny, the sort of thing that always started a movie audience to snickering. Only with him it was more than a snicker; it was laughter rolling around inside him, making no noise, just filling him to bursting with relief and joy. Why? He couldn't answer. He walked away, shaking his head from side to side. Somehow, he had been in chains and now he was free.

XII

FOR DAYS Tibby wore the moony look of one deprived of judgment. Nath became a mere shadow in the path of her dreams; she wished he would take himself away. To avoid the sight of him, she took to robbing the icebox instead of sitting down to regular meals. She couldn't stand to wait for Sunday to see Teller again, and haunted their meeting place. In vain. Was it possible he didn't feel what she did? A tremor shook her—what if even Sunday shouldn't bring him? It was easy to get out of going to church, because her father mistook leaving her alone for a way to strengthen his claim on Nath. She hurried to the glade, but Teller wasn't there and he didn't come. Where to look for a boy who used the vast sea of the Barrens for a home and never came out? As she started slowly back, her heart gathered in a knot too tight for tears.

Miles away, Teller was slaving under the one master who could strike terror to his twisted soul. Reds Truman, his father, had determined to reopen a road from the north all the way to the Red House. Where a cripple was merely soggy they had been laying beds of saplings, but a couple of deep runs called for herculean labor. Here they felled great logs, only two to each bridge. With cant hook, peavey and cracking backs they set the straight trunks parallel at the standard gauge of a truck. To the sides of the timbers they spiked lesser stringers, leaving a groove between. Thus each log became a guarded rail, equal to any load. Hard work couldn't keep Teller's mouth from watering every time he thought of Tibby. Unbelievably, she had dropped like a ripe plum, but what if she should get the idea that he had abandoned her? By Sunday morning he was desperate.

"Aw, hell, Reds," he whined, "I got somewheres to go. What's all the rush?"

"Told ye once," growled his father, "and I tell ye twice. Snoopers. I seen more'n that squirt of a gal from Yocum's, poking a long nose into nobody's business. Fixed him whilst you was down cellar, fixed him the way they stays fixed."

"Nath Storm?"

"Too fur to say."

"Dead?" whispered Teller.

"How would I know? Rifle. Think I'd ought to lay a track from here to there with my big feet!"

"They'll find him," said Teller unhappily, "and me too."

"That's how come we be overdue to clear," said Reds. "Take all our ready stuff and leave the plant behind. Happen I been too good to you, filling your pockets with bigger money'n you and me has ever seen." He squeegeed his forehead with a long finger and flicked the sweat in Teller's face. "Ain't whaled ye since Christmas," he muttered, "but now seems the time."

"What for?" quavered Teller.

"To make ye cup them big ears and hearken. You got a new sweetie, ain't ye?"

"Yeah," said Teller disconsolately; he had never been able to hide a secret from his father.

"Waal," drawled Reds, "we need a truck, a good un."

Teller's eyes flickered, searching for the connection. "You want I should steal a truck?"

"Naw, no need to," said Reds. "Old man Rinton's will

do fine." He paused. "If his own gal comes along, it won't be stealing."

Teller's gaze snapped to fixity. Slowly his lips quirked in a crooked smile. A truck without stealing, and his girl to boot! No kidding, just an everyday elopement with a borrowed truck. After that, what if he did get drafted? It made him want to laugh. "When?" he asked.

"Ye kin clear now. On your way, pull down the Yocum wire. Git going."

Returning from the woods, Tibby saw a figure crouched at the rear of the barn. She could scarcely believe her eyes, but there was no mistaking the angular knees framing a tawny torso. She wasn't aware of getting through the gate, only of coming face to face with Teller as he rose.

"Oh, Teller," she panted, "where you been all these days? When you weren't at the place today, I thought I'd die."

"Hello, Tib," drawled Teller, "you look swell." He took her in his arms and kissed her slowly. No violence to it, only a promise. "Say, Tib, I got somewhat to show ye."

"What?"

"Miles from here. We couldn't walk. Can't we take the truck?"

"Oh, I wouldn't dare. Pop will be home any minute now. Let's wait and ask him for the car. Besides, I want him to see you; what a strong hand you'd make."

"Sure," said Teller, "but that'll come later, after you seen what I want you to see. Listen, dope. If you're going to be mean about the truck, I'll fade so fast you won't know I been here."

"Aw, Teller, don't say a thing like that!"

"Do what I ask and you'll have no complaint."

"Perhaps it hasn't any gas," said Tibby hopefully.

"Plenty," said Teller, leading the way, "keys and everything. I looked." She consented, and after two turns they struck into the Friesburg Pike and headed north. Passing the store, Tibby held herself as far back in the cab as she could. Teller gave a short laugh. "Nath still got the bite on ye, eh?"

"No," she said hotly; "not even a bitty bite. Where we going, Teller?"

He lit a cigarette and let the smoke dribble from his nose, studying her slant-eyed through the haze. She was so all-fired purty, a guy couldn't hardly think. Why hadn't he questioned Reds more fully? The old man was set to clear out with two-three thousand dollars' worth of finished liquor. Then what? Was he all fixed to sell it? How long would the truck be gone? What about Tibby? Because naturally, they'd have to keep her with them. He swerved into a sandy trail so narrow that branches raked the truck on either side.

"I don't like it here," said Tibby. "I want to go back."

"Couldn't turn if you tried," said Teller, but he slowed to a stop and took her in his arms. "You scared? I'm here, ain't I? What's there to be afeard on?"

Her eyes plunged into his. "Nothing, I guess. Only it's awful hot."

He took his time kissing her before he drove on. They branched into a faint wood road under jack pines odorous from the summer heat, but the air beneath was startlingly cool. Tibby felt divided. Half of her drowsed while the other half tingled on the verge of some breath-taking plunge, yet all of her was drugged. This spot was lovely, made for dreams. Her hand went out toward Teller's knee, but she drew it back as they plunged down to a swale bedded with freshly cut saplings. Rattling across them, the truck took the rise beyond in second gear and quickly descended to the first of the two-rail bridges. Tibby snapped erect, terrified.

"Stop!" she cried. "Teller, you can't——"

Before she could finish, they were across and safe on solid ground. "What bit ye?" laughed Teller. "Didn't I promise I'd show ye somewhat?"

When they came to the next bridge, Tibby scarcely saw it, for her eyes were clamped beyond on an unforgettable excrescence of a house. On that faraway day it had presented two blind windows below, and between them a molding door. Now she looked at its hunched back and into an open lean-to that sheltered a cavernous pit. Out of it, as the truck ground to a stop, rose an apparition. The man looked twice the size of Teller and, like him, was dressed only in rolled-up pants. His hands hung almost to his knees, and the sickly yellow fuzz that coated his legs and arms deepened to red flame on his head. There was a smell to him, the same sour-sweet odor of mash and spilled liquor that hung in the air so thick that it seemed to drip from the trees.

"Hiya, Pop!" called Teller.

No gleam of welcome brightened Red's flat yellow eyes. "Turn around," he ordered, "and back up close." Jockeying the truck cleverly amid a maze of stumps, Teller finally backed it up the rise until the tailboard was level with the mouth of the black pit. Reds blocked the rear wheels. "Get out, you two."

"No," stuttered Tibby. "I want to go home."

Reds opened the door on her side and seized her wrist. Though his fingers scarcely closed, she could feel the bones begin to crack. He whipped her out, held her off and let his eyes slide down to her feet and back to her frightened face.

"Some cake," he grunted. "How the heck did Teller ever snag the likes of you?"

Teller blustered from around the truck, "Lay off, Pop!"

"Listen who says so," sneered Reds, not taking his eyes off Tibby. They were like hands, feeling her, and a red flood of color rose as if to clothe her. Reds gave a grunt of a laugh as he tossed her wrist away and faced Teller. "Beat it, and better do it quick. Take your gal home. The truck stays."

"Oh, no!" gulped Tibby. "It can't! What would I tell them? It just can't!"

"Listen, titbit," said Reds, "and I'll tell ye the whole o' what you're going to tell 'em. Learn it good, because happen your tongue should slip beyond, know what ye'll git? I'll find ye by night or day and strip the pretty meat from your bones cleaner than a buzzard picks a rabbit. Tell your folks you went for a ride with your boy friend and got mired. Tell 'em you'll get the truck out easy tomorrer morning, and not before. That's when you and Teller got to be back here."

"It's too far for her to walk," protested Teller. Reds' ham of a hand hit him a swinging blow that made him turn a cartwheel down the slope. He landed on his hands and knees, and rose slowly to his feet. "Come on, Tib," he chattered; "it won't be so far across Oxhead Woods."

She was glad to go at any price, and much sooner than she had thought possible, they had threaded a veritable web of paths and come out in sight of her house.

"I'm afraid," she whispered, "afraid to go back."

"Who'll harm ye to home?" said Teller. "Nobody. It's my old man you got to fret about. Meet me here tomorrer early. We'll fetch the truck, and when your pop finds you brought him another helper, what'll he say?"

"Oh, Teller, will you do that?" she cried. "Really?"

"Yep, you can count on it sure."

Already his mind was leaping about, dazzled by the promise of tomorrow, and hers was just as busy. Like the lightning that rips through black cloud, Reds Truman had blinded her and crammed her with terror. The truck was the link between them. Only get it back, and she need never see him again. She would be safe. She could lock herself in her room and stay safe. She started for home at a run.

XIII

TELLER made a detour to break the Yocum telephone line, then hurried back to help load casks into the truck and make all snug under a tarpaulin. "Why wait till tomorrer," he asked, "you that was in such a rush?"

Reds eyed him. "They's time I doubt I sired your wall-eyed brain," he answered. "How much start would we of had tonight with the gal along? Till supper. Tomorrer, knowing she's tangled with a mired truck, nobody'll worry short of dinner."

That night Teller scarcely slept. Dawn came at last, and an hour later he was hidden against a tree, watching for Tibby. What if she shouldn't come? His jaws clamped hard; by cripes, he'd watch his chance and snake her out by the neck. A gleam flashed through the orchard and emerged into plain sight. It was Tibby. Even from a distance, she seemed easier in her mind, and near by looked good enough to eat. A thin jersey showed her off from the waist up and a flaring short skirt did pretty well by the rest of her. Teller was hungry, and it was good to see that Tibby was carrying a block of cinnamon buns.

"Hello."

"Hiya," he answered. They broke off a couple and stood munching. "How'd you come out last night? What happened?"

"Nothing," she said with a laugh. "Can you believe it? Nobody noticed the truck's gone."

"Good," said Teller, turning into the woods.

"That ain't all," said Tibby, holding to his arm. "Saturday, Nath and Pop had an awful row, and seems Nath's quit the job."

"Hunh? What they row about?"

"Don't know, and what does it matter? All it means, Pop will be so mighty pleased to see you drive in to take Nath's place, he'll forget all about our fooling with the truck." They traveled along swiftly, both too eager to dally, but as they approached the path that led from the Yocum Farm tarn to the Friesburg Pike, a strange and mournful sound quavered from far away.

"What's that noise?"

"You plain dumb?" said Teller, scowling. "Cattle, stupe. Sounds they ain't been milked."

Abruptly he clapped his hand over her mouth and forced her to crouch. They heard the pattering of rapid feet and saw Rumble flash by with Meg holding to his chain. The dog was as intent on getting somewhere as Meg herself; she was taking great strides and sobbing as she ran. Tibby's heart pulled her two ways. She knew the recovery of the truck must come before all else, yet her lip fluttered tremulously because she wanted so much to run after Meg. Teller was changed. What had she done to make him snap at her, calling her a stupe?

"Meg," she whispered waveringly, "Meg was crying. Why?"

"Yeah," snarled Teller, "you tell me. Come along now; hang close or lose an arm. Seems we got to hurry." His voice faltered as he added, "Or—or do we?"

With Meg well out of hearing, he crossed the path at right angles, dragging Tibby along. She glanced back, trying vainly to connect Meg's distress with Nath and her father. Why had they quarreled? What about? It didn't enter her head that her own behavior had been the hidden cause. How could she know that because she had become only a nagging puzzle to her father and merely a blur to Nath, they had got to snapping like a time fuse that, in the end, had set off a bomb? They weren't conscious of the truth themselves—Mr. Rinton was totally ignorant of the existence of Teller, and Nath never stopped to figure that the reason for his hanging around no longer existed. Anyway, bang, boom and bust, leaving them both dismayed.

In his own house behind the closed store, already Nath could smile at the names he'd been called and grin over the ones he had called back. Of course, he would return to the job with not a word said on either side, but not today. Getting yourself fired had a right to pay in something better than cash—a Monday at home! Habit got him out of bed to wash, dress and eat before a sort of second sunrise flashed the glad news to his logy brain: *Stop. You don't have to burn your dogs down the road and all day long. Lie on your back with your legs sprawled wide. Take it easy. Loaf. Turn your mind out to graze.*

He did. His mind wondered lazily how his mother was getting along. It ran into Tibby kissing Teller, and that gave him a laugh. It took just one step farther back and settled down like tired bones into a feather bed—Yocum Farm. That strange habitation came alive as if he hadn't been away a day. Vision followed vision, with none of the confusion of a kaleidoscope, each picture clear and complete within itself. Pete's curses causing his silky beard to shower out like a bursting milkweed pod. Ellen's fingers gently caressing the cheek they had slapped. Poor Lot, a hub of languor to the felloe of Lottie's striding strength. Finally, there was Meg with a broken leg. Weeks ago. Apparently so helpless, yet strong enough to tangle him within a web of shame. He stared into her accusing eyes, deep as the Yocum tarn, and suddenly her crazy fears took on the clarity of forked lightning. She herself became a living presence. Not far away. Not across Oxhead Woods. Near by. Terrified. Crying out from the new depths of despair, "Nath! Nath!"

Somebody was pounding on the door, a small pounding whose intensity set the whole room to quivering. He opened, and Meg herself fell against him. His arms closed around her as if obeying a familiar impulse, but not even the hammering of her heart could persuade him he was awake until his eyes fell on Rumble. The dog was real, and so was the chain that dangled from his collar. His red eyes and his thumping tail had the eloquence of a trusting voice, friend calling to friend for aid.

"Meg!" cried Nath. "What's up?"

"Lot!" she gasped. "Lot! Oh, Nath, you're here! When I saw the smoke coming from your chimney——"

He gave her a shake. "What about Lot? Make sense, can't you?"

"Shot," she gulped. "Somebody shot him."

Nath's grip tightened on her shoulders. "Dead?"

"No. That's why you got to hurry."

"Where's he at?"

"Near the Red House."

Nath stepped into the store and came out with a hank of rope. "I'm ready. Better hang on to Rumble." They crossed the pike and entered Oxhead Woods. "How'd it happen?"

"Lot wasn't around yesterday for evening milking, nowheres. Pete went crazy, trying to telephone for help; he couldn't even raise the operator. Come eleven o'clock, the cows started to bawling, and then the heifers. Listen, you can hear them from here. We all went crazy. None of us could milk, even with Pete yelling at us how to do it. Daybreak I sneaked away with Rumble to the fields, everywhere Lot's been working. Then I remembered."

"What?"

"The day you were pestering Lottie to tell us the way to the Red House. You asked Lot how he'd like to earn——"

"Six bucks!" cried Nath.

He seized her arm. His face hardened into flint as his thoughts followed Lot through the glades of the Barrens and saw what must have happened. A rifle bullet can kill from half a mile away and leave no fingerprint, no splayfoot tracks. Coward—dirty coward! Poor Lot, who never did harm to man or beast! Meg, and now Lot. Why? Pete's mocking laughter rang in his ears. Damn Pete and his fool tales of a jumpity stone house!

"Nath, you're hurting me!"

"Which is shortest to where Lot lies," he asked, "over the broken bridge or around the upper pool?"

"Around the pool," she whimpered.

His hand went to her head, and he dragged it against his shoulder. "Aw, Meg, I'm sorry!"

He became a wall of strength that nothing could shake, a refuge. She pressed against him for a single instant, then pushed him away. "Hurry, Nath."

He went plunging through the underbrush so fast that she couldn't have kept up without Rumble's help. Once the dog yelped, and though still tugging ahead, looked back as if he were longing to go two ways at once. Nath called to him, and he straightened out, pulling harder than ever. Holding tight to the chain, twice Meg tripped and went headlong into moss and muck, but quickly scrambled to her feet. The distant plaint of the suffering Yocum herd swelled for a time, then muted as they made a turn. Choked by his collar, Rumble began to rasp louder than a blacksmith's file. Nath stopped.

"We're making too much noise," he whispered.

"Why we got to be quiet?" panted Meg. "Why?"

"Because whoever shot Lot wouldn't stop at getting us. Wait here; I got to fetch something." He slipped away through the underbrush, and was gone so long that Meg lost patience. She couldn't quite smother a moaning, a sort of crying inside. Not loud, more like the lonely whining of a puppy. In reality, Nath was gone only a short time, and returned dragging a white cedar fence rail, light but strong.

"Give me the dog," he said; "you can steady the thin end of the rail."

He was holding Rumble by his collar, forcing him to heel, when they broke into a muddy path. The dog told him which way to turn, but presently Nath stopped short, his attention seized by a triangular dent, a shallow trench that came from the left and meandered on to the right. It was fainter than the strange furrow he had noticed months ago and far away, yet he recognized that it must be a continuation. What could have made it? The answer banged through his brain, sweeping all mystery away. A metal drum. Heavy. Rolled along on its edge for miles to a hidden still.

"Dumb," he muttered; "I've been awful dumb."

"Nath," wheezed Meg, "we're almost there."

He looked at her, and at any other moment would have burst out laughing. Her arms were scratched, her tough levis torn, and her eyes peered at him mournfully out of a mask of mud. The suffering in them would have sobered him in any case. He nodded gravely and went on. When Rumble broke off the path at a sharp angle, he stopped him and motioned to Meg.

"On your hands and knees," he whispered into her ear. "Push the rail when I pull."

With Rumble ahead, Nath next, the rail on the ground and Meg for a tail, they might have been taken for a python with a broken back. It snaked along cautiously until Rumble, arriving at Lot's side, gently licked his wound as if to point it out. Lot was curled up like a dog, but when Nath touched him he straightened, opened his eyes and smiled.

"Knowed you'd come," he breathed.

There was only a slight puncture where the bullet had entered just above the right lung, but a great hole gaped where it had come out through the back. The binding of Lot to the rail, face up and nearer one end than the other, so Nath could carry two-thirds of the load, was slow work. At last it was done, the entire hank of rope forming a huge cocoon that bulged where Nat's jumper had been wadded inside for a cushion under Lot's neck. So far nobody had risen, but now Nath straightened from the knees and looked around, trying to figure from what direction the bullet could have come. There was no clear vista; Lot must have crawled away from the spot where he was shot. Nath was about to move to get a better look when Rumble swirled to his feet, every muscle quivering and hackles stiff. There was a hiatus of breathless silence before Nath made a snatch for his chain and missed.

"Catch him!" he cried sharply. "Hold him!"

Too late; Meg also missed. Already Rumble had shot forward and was tearing in a straight line through the brush with the loose chain thrashing behind him.

"Oh!" she wailed.

"Come on!" shouted Nath. "Noise don't matter now!"

He shouldered the heavier end and she the lighter. From behind them, already far away, came a tangle of sounds. A rushing. The crack of a rifle. A yelp of fury. The rifle again. Finally, a mad mingling of the clamor of battle, man against dog. From ahead, growing ever louder, rose the bedlam of the suffering cows.

"Rumble!" called Meg weakly, more a sob than a cry. "Rumble!"

"Ease off, Meg," said Nath. "He gave us our chance, didn't he? Shouldn't wonder he's saved your life and mine, along with what's left of Lot's. It's up to you and me to finish the job."

That steadied her, and an hour of silence passed before they reached the edge of the tarn. Meg thought their troubles were over, but Nath knew the worst was before them. The ancient paving of the ramp wasn't only grass-grown; it was treacherous with layers of moss that turned into slippery oil under pressure. They had to dig in with their toes to make sure of each step before they dared take another. As they topped the rise, the full blast of bawling from the barn engulfed them like a comber. Before Lottie's door, they set their burden down and knelt beside it. Slowly they raised their heads and stared into each other's eyes.

"I'll go for the doc," murmured Nath, "whilst you tell Lottie."

Fear ripped through Meg, setting her to shaking. "No!" she sobbed. "Tell her yourself. You know he's dead."

Nath opened the door. Lottie was kneeling in the center of the cabin with her big Bible open on a settle before her. Her head wasn't bowed; straight as a poker she was calling upon her God, demanding aid in words so rapid that they telescoped into a steady stream. Nath had to touch her shoulder to make her stop. The best thing to do was to tell the truth, half of it anyway.

"We brought Lot back," he announced.

"Lot?" She sprang to her feet and looked around wildly. When her eyes fell to the great cocoon lying outside, she uttered a cry that topped all other sounds and seemed to pierce the very sky. "Lot, my son!"

They carried him in, rail and all, and laid him on her bed. Nath stopped only to slash the rope in half a dozen places and tell Meg to get Dr. Byrne anyway, then he rushed to the barn. Not even bothering with a pail, he milked like mad, enough to relieve each cow. He felt like kicking the silly heifers. What had they to bawl about? He could have hugged the placid bull, bright-eyed, but massively indifferent.

The general clamor dwindled and ceased; that job was done. As he came out, he almost collided with Pete, carrying a shotgun.

"What for?" asked Nath. "Me?"

Pete stared at him blankly. "The noise. The bawling and bellering. All night and all day. Druv us crazy. No help from anywheres. Ellen racing about the house, stopping her ears and screaming for me to shoot the critters, shoot 'em all." His face took on a babyish look, as if about to dissolve in tears. "Now I gone deef. Never heard ye come nor can't hear the hollering no more."

"You ain't deaf," said Nath; "I milked 'em enough to stop their noise. Let's have the gun; maybe I got a use for it."

As Pete released his hold, he seemed to come awake. "Nath! Eh, Nath!"

"Sure," said Nath unsmilingly. "Who'd you think it was?"

Benignity flooded Pete's face, wiping out trouble and the memory of their angry parting. "You're back! You've come home!"

"Yeah," said Nath with a frown, "I guess that's right."

He had a feeling of being owned. His weeks away appeared to vanish from time. Even the store, scene of his boyhood, became reduced to the level of a telephone booth where anybody with a nickel to spend had a right to enter. There he had been a child, here he had become a man. It was as though Yocum Farm, with its vague terrors and strange assortment of persons, possessed a lushness near to violence that asked only months to bind your soul tight as baling wire.

The conviction worked two ways, commanding him to take charge. "Go tell Miss Ellen she can quit worrying," he ordered.

"Sure, sure," agreed Pete meekly, and went toddling off.

Nothing could have proved quicker to what a pass things at the farm had come than the change in Pete, who once had been able to see and hear through walls. Now you could carry a dead man past his nose and he not know it. Nath entered the cabin. Rail and cord gone, Lot lay extended on the bed with Lottie leaning over him. She had cut away his jumper and was sponging his inert body with a liquid that looked like tea. Meg came in, breathless.

"Had to go down to Parker's on the County Road to phone. Telephoned everywhere for Doc Byrne. Out on his calls. His office promised to send him soon as ever they could catch him."

Nath stared toward the bed blankly, wondering why all the rush. "Is Lot alive?"

"Lottie acts she thinks so, but even if he isn't——"

"You got good sense, Meg," Nath broke in. "What about the troopers? You call them too?"

"No. I guess I was dumb, after all."

Lottie's hand hung suspended and she spoke without turning. "Wasn't it you done it, Nath?"

Nath was too astonished to answer, but Meg cried out, "Are you crazy? This wasn't any accident, only we don't know who did do it."

"Where'd it happen?" asked Lottie sharply.

Meg hesitated. "The Red House—near the Red House."

Lottie writhed to her feet and faced them. In an instant she became transformed, her blue eyes blazing out of a face suddenly contorted. Straight and incredibly tall, she raised both fists and seemed to hammer the unseen sky.

"No use!" she wailed, kicking aside the basin of liquid. "Curse you, Hube Snell! May the Lord hold your black heart forever in the nethermost pit of hell!" She collapsed into a chair, a shriveled old woman. Burying her face in her hands, she swayed back and forth, and her voice, a moment before so strong, became a keening moan. "Oh, Lot, my son, the mark is on ye!"

Meg laid a hand on her shoulder. "Don't, Lottie. Please don't."

Instinctively Lottie swept her into her lap and drew her close to her heart, but her swaying only slowed. "Aie, aie!" she moaned. "My son, stabbed by my own hand! Who am I to condemn? Whose was the sin of silence? Mine. Silence hath sold my son beyond bondage unto death. Listen, you two. Hear all and tell all. Let the flood of the truth cleave me like a parted wall, so you can look through and see them happy days."

"Aw, Lottie," said Nath, sinking on a bench and laying the gun on the floor, "you had nought to do with it; no more had Hube Snell."

"Though Hube be dead," declared Lottie, "the evil of him lives on and walks. I could've stopped it had I hearkened to the cry of God: 'Vengeance is mine.' Three of us there was, the age that you be now. Pete, Ellen and me, grown strong at the same breast, and Pete with a laugh so clear it could carry to Burden Hill, where Elspeth lived. Like doe to buck, she answered its call, shy feet but a bold heart. In that happy time, joy echoed up and down the tarn, across the fields and through the woods. Dogwood, lilac and orchard blooms in May. Lupin racing cornflowers for the deepest blue in June. Chinquapins shaking their pale yaller kitten tails as we passed. Aye, all was well until love laid its knot on Elspeth and Pete."

"Pete?" exclaimed Meg wonderingly. "He's so awful fat!"

"He wasn't then. My, no! He had the looks and the strength of Nath himself. His hand against Elspeth's waist could swing her across the widest run. But the love of others is a contágion. Looking upon it, a young girl can drink poison with her eyes. So with Ellen. In love with love, she turned her back on the rest of us and set herself to roam. Wide, far and farther, but in the end always daring the paths that led close to the Red House and Hubert Snell."

"Is it her that screams?" breathed Meg.

"No; Ellen laughed and later wept, but never screamed. Hubert was mighty of strength and small of heart. His arms had the greed of a rooting hog. Like a black spider he was wont to wait in his web, and not even the stirring of his unborn child had the power to drag him forth to make all well with Ellen. Elspeth couldn't believe no man could be so heartless. Alone she slipped away to plead with Hubert, and never more returned."

"Why wouldn't she?" said Nath angrily.

Lottie balanced her head hopelessly. "Where be the words to lift the blindness from your eyes? Ellen, dark and tiger-strong. Elspeth, bright and frail as the shaft of sunlight you can cut short with your hand. Alone with Hubert in the Red House. No ear to hear, no hand to help, believing no evil. One minute brimming with faith and purity, the next a torn and emptied cup. Can a lamb cleanse itself of its own blood? Bearing what gift would she come back to Pete?"

"It's she that screams," whispered Meg.

"Night and day," said Lottie. "Ellen would've growed to be a match for Hubert, and he knew it, but Elspeth promised a lifelong feast for his greed. He was eager and quick to marry her helplessness, binding her to him with the merciless cord of the law. Then it was that her screams destroyed silence forever."

"Pete," said Nath, coloring darkly, "what did he do?"

"For a time, a madness fell on him. He wandered all the Barrens, circling the Red House from afar, creeping within hearing and rushing away. He held 'twas the house that moved, not he. Chasing him, hounding. Already his mother was nigh spent with her breast ailment, but to Pete her pain stood for nought. She died, and swift after her his father, yet Pete shed no tear. As master of Yocum Farm, a blackness entered his heart. It turned him shrewd as a weasel, and belly to the ground he made a dealing with Hubert Snell."

"Oh!" cried Meg, lifting her head.

"Pete crawling who had never crawled," continued Lottie. "Humbling himself before Hubert. Whining how would he work the farm alone. Declaring he could stand no longer the nearness of Elspeth. In the end, they made their deal—Hube to bring six thousand dollars in cash and Pete to sign away the farm. Sign any writing whatever, witnessed by Ellen and me. Only it must be at night and secret, that none should discover Ellen's approaching shame."

Meg hid her face. "Ellen!" she whispered dumbly.

"Hube came on a winter night of storm," continued Lottie, "ice heavy on the slopes, and branches cracking loud as pistol shots. The steaming horses pulling on their bits, glad of level ground. The surrey, curtained like a hearse against the cold. Pete rushing out the front door, a bull whip in his hand. The crack of the whip, sharper than the cracking of the trees and stabbing the team with a dart of flame."

Lottie sprang to her feet, forgetting Meg, who rolled to the floor, and the voice that now came out of her had the sound of the shout of a man. "Drive right around! Drive right around and in!" She uttered a cackle of laughter and strode up and down, clapping her hands. Meg crept to sit beside Nath and he slipped an arm around her. The look of Lottie's face dragged their eyes from their heads. "Them horses," she chortled, "hitting the top of the ramp at a run!"

"Into the tarn," whispered Nath hoarsely.

"No, sir!" cried Lottie wildly. "Not with the ramp banked the way it is, not with the icehouse doors wide open! Looked like a stable to beast and man, wouldn't it? Then Pete—Pete——" Her lips trembled weakly and her jaw sagged. "No," she muttered, "I can't, I can't!"

"Go on," commanded Nath, tightening his grip on Meg.

Lottie's teeth chattered and her staring eyes took on a glaze. "No. Not that; only what come after will I tell ye. Pete running all the way to the Red House to assure Elspeth she need nevermore fear. Aie, what did he find? Elspeth could of stood forever the cruelest beating at the hands of Hube Snell, but not the belief that Pete had turned his back on her undying grief."

"What——" began Meg. "What——" she repeated.

"You can look it up in the sheriff's office forty-nine year ago," muttered Lottie, "how they found Elspeth dead and Hubert gone with all his cash. Sleet turned to rain, cleansing the tracked snow, and Hube they never found—never!"

"The horses?" questioned Nath.

Lottie's eyes came alive and shrewd. "Them neither." She gave an odd snicker and continued, "The icehouse floor give way that night. How? Beams sawed halfway through by Pete's own hand caused floor and all to pitch into ten foot of muck. Nobody suspicioned Yokum Farm afore or after the search, not even when all the county come to Pete's sale. At the vendue, he held back only a team and wagon, and we closed the house. Then began our pilgrimage, and it was me done the guiding to the home of the Dark People where I was born. But sin traveled with us, the sin of silence. A year—a whole year of tribulation afore three young people, turned hard and old, come back to Yocum Farm. Did I say three? Three and two more, one at the breast and Lot unborn." She staggered and sank on her knees beside the bed. "Blood was spilled and never paid, save by my guiltless boy. O Lord, how oft have my lips opened to lift the curse of the Red House, yet ever did my faith lose holt on Thy mercy, O my Redeemer!"

Meg stood up, trembling violently "Lottie," she cried, "the other baby! Ellen's—Ellen's baby. What became of it?"

Lottie turned her head slowly. "She married Ben Yarrow and died the day she gave birth to you."

Meg made a strangled sound, and Nath was quick to rise and take her in his arms. He had thought only to comfort her, but something got in the way—himself. This Meg wasn't a kid in trouble, running to him for help. What his arms held was neither girl nor woman, but himself, his own heart and blood. If there be aught above and beyond love, this was it. Plain as writing on a wall, he stared at the certainty that he and Meg were partners in the breath of life, share or die. There was no mush to it, only sureness. Where had it come from? When had it started? He couldn't answer. Only one thing was crystal clear—it was here to stay.

XIV

"LET'S GO, Meg," said Nath. "You can run tell Ellen about Lot while I hike down to telephone the sheriff."

"No," said Meg, clinging to him. "Please, Nath. Please come with me. Just for a minute."

Outside, Nath made her stop at the pump. Just as she had worked the handle for him ages ago, now he did it for her, but first he knocked the caked mud from her levis and shirt. She rolled up her sleeves as high as they would go, bathed her arms and then her face. When she was through, the golden brown of her skin seemed to smile, but not her eyes. They were deep, and still clouded with a swirl of wonder. There was no towel. Nath took out a big handkerchief; not satisfied with merely drying her, he cleaned up what she had missed.

"You look fine," he said encouragingly; "purty enough to eat."

When they entered the big kitchen, it was a shock to find everything unchanged. As if they had stepped back to before Nath's quarrel with Pete—farther, back of Meg's broken leg. Pete was hunching his chair to the end of the table and Ellen had just laid out the midday meal. Meg felt cut in two, part of her breathing a natural air and the rest thrashing around like the severed tail of a snake. Sundown—snakes don't die till sundown. Would she have to wait that long, grow still and become whole once more before she could rise as a new person, daughter to Ellen's daughter? Like an automaton, Ellen set two more places. The peace on her face and Pete's seemed to belong not to them alone, but to the whole room and all who entered.

Even Pete's voice shared its universal bounty. "Set, and welcome."

Meg hung back, her wide eyes fastened with such intensity on Ellen that she turned as if somebody had called her name. "Well?" she said. The richness of her tone, the kindliness that softened the austerity of her lean face, both struck the exact note familiar to all of Meg's remembered life—until today. "What you staring at so hard?" continued Ellen with a flicker of a smile. "My dress buttoned crooked?"

"No," stammered Meg. Letting go of Nath, she ran to throw her arms around Ellen's waist and press her face hard against her.

"My, my!" said Ellen. "Why you shaking so?"

Meg couldn't tell her the real reason, not yet. "Lot," she said in a smothered voice. "Lot's been shot."

"Where's he at?" asked Ellen quickly.

"On Lottie's bed," said Nath. "I got to notify the sheriff."

"Eh?" grunted Pete. "How's that?"

Ellen forced Meg to sit down, and turned to Nath. "You too," she said. "Eat a bite while I go to Lottie."

The steaming food seemed to breed a momentary forgetfulness; Meg ate slowly and Nath with a rush. He was about ready to quit anyway when he heard a hooting from down the lane. He ran out, followed by Meg. The man who climbed from the car seemed a stranger, incredibly aged. In a matter of weeks, overwork had cut the lines in Dr. Byrne's face so deep that he couldn't have smiled if he tried.

"Well, what now?" he asked wearily, starting for the main house.

"This way, doc," said Nath.

They led him inside the cabin, and as he approached the

bed Pete's bulk filled the door. "Get out of the light," begged the doctor, "please!" Pete squeezed through and moved into a dark corner as Dr. Byrne opened his bag and went to work. "Why wasn't I called sooner?" he asked without turning. "Why'd you move him? I'd have thought you'd have better sense."

"You couldn't have got to where he lay," said Nath, "not without you walked through mud and water and tore your clothes."

"Where would that be?" asked Pete eagerly.

"Nigh to the source of your sin," cried Lottie in a loud voice, "the Red House!" She glared at Ellen. "And yours too! Who was it welcomed the seed of unlawful life? Who sowed dragon's teeth, condemning the innocent to reap the crop of death?"

"Stop your fuss!" said Dr. Byrne impatiently. "This man was shot. How? Who did it?"

"I could guess," said Nath, "but guesses don't count when it comes to murder."

The doctor straightened. "Have you called the sheriff?"

"No," said Nath, coloring. "Telephone's down and I was just starting to the Parkers' when you came. I'll go now."

"Leave it to me and save time," said the doctor; "I'm about through here." He pressed open the larger wound, sifted into it a generous handful of pale yellow powder and strapped a bandage in place. "That's all for now. I'll notify the state police as well as the sheriff."

"Will Lot live?" asked Ellen quietly. "Isn't that what matters most?"

"Miracles sometimes happen," said Dr. Byrne on his way out; "let's hope for one now."

The shotgun, lying on the floor, caught Nath's attention.

He frowned. Why had he taken it from Pete? What had he wanted it for? Was it loaded? What if somebody should kick the trigger? He picked it up and broke the breech; the gun was loaded, all right, with heavy shot. Still frowning, he hurried out and started straight across the fields to the south, almost at a run. Meg caught up with him.

"Nath! Where you going?"

"To search for Rumble. Perhaps he'll give me more than guessing to tell the troopers when they come. You better run along home, Meg."

"No," she said.

He didn't argue, neither did he slacken his pace, stepping high through dewberry vines. They were mean, anchored at both ends. Meg tripped and had to race to save herself. He didn't laugh, and kept on going.

"Seems I'm always falling," she panted.

"You can take it," he said, "broken leg and all. Don't it hurt none?"

"Not a bit; stronger than it ever was. Say, this ain't the way to where we found Lot!"

"No," said Nath, "but straight ahead will cross the line between there and the Red House, won't it?"

They climbed the outermost fence of Yocum Farm and plunged through the woods Here the going underfoot was easier, but you had to watch out for the rigid branches of the scrub oaks and the stabbing needles of jack pines. They left the high land, descended beneath great trees and came to a deep run. Nath stepped into the water. Holding the gun away with one hand, he placed the other behind Meg's waist and swept her across to the farther bank.

"My," she said, "like—like Pete with Elspeth!"

Nath didn't answer. He was staring at a leaf, lying close

to her feet. He climbed out, picked it up, rubbed it. His eyes studied the ground, first in the direction he had been traveling and then toward the north. After a long pause he turned north and walked along slowly. Intent, his head low, he followed the stream.

They had gone some distance before Meg cried out, "Nath, stop! Isn't that blood? Oh, here's——"

"Go back!" he ordered. "Get back!"

Too late to save her from a first look, he pulled her face against his breast to blot out the ghastly sight, but no power on earth would ever erase from her mind what she had glimpsed. Rumble, mangled and dead. Not only in blood was the story written but in flaking bits of flesh and bone. Using his forelegs alone, he had dragged what was left of his haunches in and out of the water, reviving himself, fighting to the last to get home and tell his tale.

Meg wasn't crying; it was worse than that. As if her body had been riven apart and emptied, she seemed scarcely to breathe. She began to shake violently. Half a mile back, Nath had hesitated between going south to the Red House for a showdown and following Rumble's bloody trail. Now he had to choose again. He let the gun slide to the ground; Meg must come first always, ahead of all else. He lifted her and went crashing away from that spot. A branch lashed him across the eyes, and he was glad of it; it forced him to look ahead and not back. Out of breath, he sank on a bank of moss with Meg across his knees. No sound had come from her and she was shaking worse than ever.

Smoothing her hair, he began to talk. "He did a good job. Man nor dog can do more than give his life for a friend."

Meg turned toward him, hiding her face. "He loved me,"

she said brokenly; "he belonged to me. My own grandmother never told me who I really was. Pete has scared me all my life. Lottie's bound to hate me for finding the Red House. Only Rumble loved me. Nobody's ever been mine but Rumble."

Nath kept smoothing her head. "I love you, Meg. I'm yours for all my life, if you'll have me."

"You're not!" she cried, struggling to free herself. "You're saying that just because I'm miserable. You belong to Tibby."

He clamped his elbow across her waist, holding her down. "Tibby?" he said vaguely. "Oh, yeah. But you're wrong."

"I'm not! Everybody knows it! Let me go! I hate you!"

He caught both her wrists in one hand and shook her. "Listen, can't you? I'm through with Tibby, been through with her for days as long as years. It's you I love, Meg."

"Since when?" she asked quietly.

"I found it out today."

Her calm had fooled him into relaxing his hold. Before he could stop her, she was on her feet and running. He followed slowly, forgetful of the gun. When he crossed the boundary into Yocum Farm, he stopped and gazed across the neglected fields. They didn't belong to Meg; perhaps they never would. But quite aside from his love for her, they talked to his heart. It wasn't a question of pay; he'd willingly work from dawn to dark in trade for the joy of bringing them back to fullness and life. Feed the land and the land will feed you. That truth was as old as the hills, and never in all time had a hungry world cried louder for help from those who work the soil.

Arriving at Lottie's cabin, he was about to go in when he heard a dull clamor issuing from the main house that chilled his bones. He dashed through the grape arbor, crossed the lean-to in a stride and burst into the big kitchen. What he saw anchored all his muscles, stopping him cold. Meg backed into a corner, her eyes wide with fright. The iron point of Pete's trench stick embedded in a wall, its staff still quivering like a thrown spear. Pete! Pete using his hands for extra feet to steady his tiny feet on the floor. The hands were walking along the edge of the great table, and directly opposite them Ellen, her face as bloodless as death. Catlike, she was matching the pace of the hands step for step, keeping the table evenly between herself and Pete.

Out of his throat rolled disjointed words, glued together by the hate of years. "Told her—you that ne'er would let me tell! Who kept me from washing the blood from my soul? You! Who would have told long years ago? Me! You, thief of my sole salvation, tattling and telling all! You, the source of every grief! Where's Elspeth? Where's me that was? Lost! Dead afore I ever lived! Who led me to kill? Damn ye! Wait for me! Dare ye! One hand—only one!"

"It wasn't me that told," whispered Ellen, measuring a step to each word.

"Liar!" shouted Pete. "Heerd ye! Heerd ye tell Meg that Lottie spoke true!" He was having no glazed, unseeing fit; his eyes blazed with conscious fury. As Ellen reached the exact middle of the table opposite him, his hands left its top to clamp under its edge. With a mighty heave, he tipped it upward and flattened her against the wall. "Hi!" he screamed. "Hi!"

Nath was freed at last. He leaped forward, swept his leg like a scythe and knocked Pete's toddling feet from under him. He fell with a thud that shook the house.

XV

BACK, go back. Back of Pete getting his pins bowled from under him. Back of Lottie's story. Back to before Nath and Meg had carried Lot home. Back to when Rumble, Meg and Nath were starting out from the store while Tibby and Teller were still cowering from their glimpse of the passing dog and sobbing girl. Although Tibby had lived all her life next door to the Barrens, they still baffled her as they have baffled many a man for years on end. For her to enter them was always a daring adventure that would turn into a nightmare should she have to find her way out alone. She had learned the route to her trysting place with Teller, drawn by a force that was stronger than fear. But this vast triangular region between Yocum Farm, the Storms' store and the Red House was as foreign to her and as menacing as the Everglades of Florida.

Since she wasn't alone, why was she uneasy? What's intuition? What good does it do? Can it tell you that if your eyes could sweep a mile instead of a measly five yards, you would stand stark as a swamp-killed tree, forever blasted by fear? She wasn't the only one. She could feel the fear in Teller. His movements were as uncertain as his dodging mind. Asking him questions. Kicking his insides around. Turning him sick with having to think. Who was it Reds had killed? Pete? One of them straight-haired darkies? Anyways, somebody from over to Yocum's or the cows wouldn't be bawling. Why get yourself muxed up with your old man's private murder? What if you didn't? How long would your own neck stay whole?

Right at the start, as they crossed the path where Rumble and Meg had just passed on their way to look for Nath, Tibby noticed that it was well beaten and must lead somewhere. She hated to leave it behind and only the thought of the truck kept her from turning back to run after Meg. It surprised her that Teller seemed no longer in a hurry; he dawdled along, frowning and muttering to himself. She tried lagging behind to see if he would notice, but he didn't. Once he disappeared from sight for a moment, and promptly panic seized her as she realized that already they were fairly deep into the untracked wilderness. She ran straight forward, and would have kept on going if she hadn't heard a short laugh off to the side. It was Teller, sitting with his back against the trunk of the enormous beech near the black pool. She strolled over and faced him angrily.

"What's the catch?" she asked. "For half of two cents I'd slap your face."

"Try it," said Teller, looking up at her mockingly. But his reddish eyes couldn't hold; they kept shifting as if he were trying to think of six things at once. "Aw, sit down."

"I won't. We've—we've got to get the truck."

A sharp yelp from far away cut through the still air, followed by a quieting call. Teller's hand shot out, seized her wrist, and by a downward pressure forced her to crumple at his side. "Hush," he whispered. "Listen!"

She pressed against him. "What is it?" she whispered.

"People walking," he murmured almost inaudibly. "Keep quiet."

Soon she could distinguish the crunching of twigs, the snapping of a dead branch, the rasping of choked breath. None of these sounds was near. They were individual, given form by the silence all around, and in the end each dropped away like a spent bullet. Only an indistinct crackling persisted, and even that grew steadily fainter and died. Teller had been tense as a taut wire; now he relaxed and her shoulder could feel warmth returning to his body. His right hand caressed her arm lazily.

"They've gone," he said, not bothering to keep his voice low. "Give me one of them buns."

She broke off two, one for herself. "Who d'you suppose it was?" she asked.

"Nath, Meg and the Yocum dog," said Teller.

"Why? How d'you know?"

"I ain't bright, but you're dumber," he jeered. "How wouldn't anybody know?"

Angry again, she drew away, but he pulled her back easily, settling her firmly against himself. She gave up struggling. "What's come over you, Teller? Why're you so mean?"

His hand worked up and down her arm absently. "Don't aim to be mean," he said. "It's having to think gets me riled—always did and always will."

"About what?"

"Which way to go, back along of you or forrards into trouble. What road to take."

"You ain't lost, are you?" said Tibby incredulously. "Can't you find the way to the truck?"

"Sure. Easy. But happen I don't want no truck with no truck." He laughed shortly at his own joke. "Happen you and me might do better to head the other way, hitch-hike to Elkton and get ourselves married."

"But—but what about Pop's truck?"

"Aw, forget it! Once we be tied good and proper, what can your old man do?"

"No, no!" said Tibby, struggling to rise. To her surprise

he let her go, and she started off aimlessly. She hadn't taken ten steps before she realized her folly. She couldn't even decide from what direction they had come, much less read a track. She went back to Teller. He hadn't moved except to pluck a blade of three-square. He was crumpling one end of it and chewing the other, his eyes staring straight ahead. "Get up!" she said sharply. "You show me the way to the truck or I'll start screaming my head off."

"Go ahead," said Teller, "scream your guts out for all I care."

She sank on her knees before him and changed her tactics. "Oh, Teller, please be nice the way you used to be!"

His eyes slipped down her tight jersey to her wide skirt, avoiding her face. Slowly his hands went around her waist and he drew her across his lap. He started kissing her, a queer sort of kissing. It had no ardor and no drive to it; more as if he were trying to forget his worries and escape from himself. Out of the distance, piercing through a mile of quiet, came the crack of a rifle, once—twice. Teller surged to his feet, rolling her to the ground. He stood hunched over, his bat ears actually twitching with the intensity of their listening to a bestial distant uproar, mysterious as thunder on a cloudless day. Even after it had ceased, he didn't move for what seemed an age.

"It's—it's stopped," said Tibby.

"One of 'em's finished," he muttered. "Wonder which?"

"What you talking about?" she asked, getting to her feet.

"None of your business." Which had won out, he asked himself, Reds or the dog? It made a lot of difference, for who would dare double-cross Reds Truman alive? Not him, so he had to find out. He started forward, stepping cautiously. "Foller if you like, but make no noise or I'll lam ye."

Tibby discovered she had grown afraid of Teller, yet she was more afraid of staying alone. With catlike stealth she followed him, her footfall so silent that it ended by fooling him. He turned around curiously and was startled to find her so close that his shoulder brushed her. He grunted and went on, traveling a little faster. They walked a long way, growing hotter every minute. She had to keep her eyes on Teller, and the sheen of sweat rippling down his back intensified the maddening itch of her own neck.

At last they came to the verge of the woods, and Teller threw out an arm to stop her. They peered from behind a screen of leaves at a stagnant pond. Its left bank rose shallowly and then with a steep sweep into the pinkish blob of the Red House. The Dutch apron over its lower windows had corroded into a mangy eyebrow, and guttering rain had bracketed the door below with streaks like tobacco juice.. Following them down, Tibby's eyes discovered a monstrous toad at the water's edge. Reds Truman! Squatting on his heels. Soaking a sweat rag in the pond and sopping a wound in his neck that had torn the flesh off his right jaw. Teller's arm stayed rigid across her front, warning her to keep still. Calculation was in his rudderless brain. Sneak away? Go boldly forward? Which? A sudden inspiration made him want to laugh. He seized Tibby's wrist and forced her to rush forward with him.

"Hiya, Pop!" he cried breathlessly. "Eh, what happened to ye?"

Reds stood up. Not only his neck was torn. One shoulder had been savagely bitten, and gaping tears in his trousers showed where his legs had been raked by claws.

Curses rumbled out of his throat. At first they were hoarse, indistinct, like somebody relearning to talk. Then they grew shrill and clear, calling every vile name he could drag from the sinkhole of his past, daring Teller to come forward and double-daring him to run.

"Aw, shut up!" yelled Teller. "Was it my fault I had to wait? Take it out on the girl, not me! Standing me up for an hour! What if I'd come back without her?"

"I wasn't late!" choked Tibby, breaking loose. "He's lying!"

Reds started for Teller with swinging arms. Tibby's first thought was to get away from the sight of the fight, and sheer instinct told her to run around the house, not try to go back the way she'd come. The truck—she remembered the truck! There it stood, unrecognizable under its bulging load. Only her father's name across the door of the cab—R. P. RINTON, FARMER—could persuade her it was the same. She climbed in, pressed the starter and eased the brake. In spite of the slant, the truck didn't budge. She had forgotten the blocked wheels. She set the emergency, scrambled out and fell on her hands and knees. Only panic gave her the strength to tug the stones away, one and then the other. No brake ever made could have held against that load, and slowly the truck began to move. She made a leap for the running board just as the Trumans, summoned by the noise of the motor, came pounding around the house.

"Steer it!" screamed Teller. "Steer!"

It didn't enter her head to steer from the running board and she lost time getting behind the wheel Hitting the steeper grade, the emergency quit altogether, and though she threw all her weight on the foot brake, the truck quickly gained speed.

Red's great voice hammered into her head, "Mesh them gears!"

She tried in vain; the whirling sprocket seemed to shatter her arm to the shoulder. She looked ahead. The narrow troughs along the logs of the spider bridge spelled safety—hit them clean and she could surely escape. She hadn't the brains to know it; all the troughs did was to fill her with terror, and she actually steered to miss them. The front wheels plunged over the bank and the truck all but turned a somersault. The wheel knocked the wind from her body, and when she came to, the first thing she heard was Teller's voice, "Don't kill her, Pop; we ain't got time."

"You're right," said Reds, choking back his rage, "more right'n you know. Fetch shovels! Git out the jack!"

For an hour Tibby cowered behind the wheel, her brain a whirling ache. How could she ever have fallen for Teller? But it was his blood-soaked father that froze her heart. She knew every minute was giving her some chance to get away, only she didn't have the sense to see how. She could blow the horn with all her might. Then what? She shuddered. Right now both men were busy unloading casks at the rear, soon they would go to the front to work at jacking up the mired wheels. *Don't be a coward. Slip out. Creep across one of the logs on hands and knees. Then run. Won't you have the ruts the truck made only yesterday to guide you? Run till you drop.* She slipped to the ground noiselessly. Using the truck for a screen, on all fours she reached one of the logs and crept along it. Her heart began to pound. It was going to work; she was almost across!

Reds stood watching her through the glass in the back of the cab; he needed a rest anyway. One end of his loose mouth tipped up in a smile, but his eyes stayed as hard as a cat's with a mouse. When Tibby had only a yard to go, he stepped around the truck and ran nimbly the full length of the other log. She didn't hear or see him until she sprang joyfully to her feet, ready to run.

"Don't touch me!" she chattered hoarsely. "If you do, I'll shout so loud ——"

"Shout, will ye?" said Reds, seizing her shoulder. "I'll give ye what for to shout!" Her throat locked as he slapped her face this way and that, raking his filthy hand, rough as a file, back and forth as he had done with Meg. Her head rolled loosely from side to side. She was inert; she couldn't even sob. Throwing her over his shoulder, he walked back across the log and pushed her into the slanted seat of the truck. "Stay there! Move or squeak and I'll wring your neck!"

The truck was unloaded; now to raise the front wheels high enough so the motor base would clear. Time, thought Reds, how could he save time and his own neck? Teller had turned up an hour late, and along of a flyweight girl already two more precious hours had been lost. Three hours chucked clean away! He swung and slapped Teller off his feet. He stayed down, knee bent like a sprinter on his marks.

"What for?" he whined.

"To make ye step," grunted Reds. "Git out block and tackle! Rig a fall and we'll haul her out!"

Thirty more minutes passed, each loaded with its portent of win or die. At last they were set to pull. No other two men could have bettered that strain. The rivulet of blood trickling from the wound in Red's neck spurted into a stream as he gave the final terrific heave that dragged the truck out with a jerk. But that same jerk parted a strand of rope and sent Teller and his father tumbling backward, Reds let out an agonized scream, "Block her!"

Too late; like a stubborn pig, the truck returned to plunge into its wallow. Teller began to cry, blubbering sobs from a giant baby. Reds stood with his hands hanging to just above his knees, a glassy stare in his yellow eyes.

"It's all to do over," he said quietly. "Next time we'll have the gal stand ready to block."

XVI

LEAVING Yocum Farm, Dr. Byrne failed to turn at the end of the long lane and was just in time to stop his car from plunging into a ditch He looked around dazedly. He was blocking the wrong side of the County Road. Luckily it was lonely, slicing across the Barrens in a long straight line. He backed around, his hands trembling violently. He had gone to sleep. Only the jounce as he left the lane had saved him. He drew up at the side of the road to steady himself. Any man as tired as he was had no right to drive. He was pinch-hitting for three younger doctors, gone to war, and the thought of his office made him shudder. More calls, more cases of other people's lives and deaths. What about himself? Dead, what good would he be to anybody? Here was a good place to snatch a nap. No nurse, no telephone. Telephone? Lot. The police! He dreamed that he turned on the ignition and pressed the starter. The dream was so real that he sank back with a satisfied sigh and slept.

In the Yocum kitchen, Nath was helping Pete get up. "You're going to bed," he said, "with the door locked from the outside."

"Huh!" sputtered Pete. "Who says so?"

"I do," said Nath. "Want me to leave you again? Say so and I'll be on my way."

Pete seemed to crumple. "No, boy, no!"

Ellen slipped from between the table and the wall. "Let him go, Nath. I'm not afraid of him." She cast a quick glance at Meg. "If it wasn't for Meg, I would of let him catch me long ago."

As Nath righted the table, Meg woke from her stunned trance. "Don't say that!" She looked questioningly at Pete, already trundling toward his chair. "Pete," she said, "Pete, you wouldn't really——"

Pete settled himself with a ludicrous wiggle. "All's done as needs to be done," he declared. "Soon's the word you folks has started gits to rolling, the sheriff'll come to fotch me sure, Fifty year ago they'd o' hung me by my thin neck till dead, God save your soul. Now seems how the law's changed. So's my neck, plenty changed, plenty."

"All you need do is keep your own mouth shut," said Ellen, "and nobody'll come to fetch you now or ever."

The routine of a farm has a grip city folk can't picture. Chores, food, work, sleep and chores again, clank along as irresistibly as the treads on a tractor. Ellen found food, though nobody ate much. Nath asked her to call him if anything happened, and went out for a real milking, taking Meg along to fetch and carry. Where he had finished, he was astonished the sheriff hadn't yet shown up. He found a flashlight and a bit of wire in the lean-to, and started out. He had spoken scarcely a word during the milking, and neither had Meg; now she ran after him.

"What you going to do?"

"Follow the phone wire. Perhaps it's between here and the County Road that it's down."

"Want me to come along?"

"Suit yourself," he answered shortly.

Twilight turned into near night when they entered the lane beyond the drawgate. With the aid of the flashlight, Nath spotted the trees that served as telephone poles and discovered the break. It was where the line was deepest hidden by the woods, and handing the light to Meg, he straddled a branch and spliced the wire as high as he could reach. When he dropped to the ground, she cut the switch and the sudden gloom hid them from each other.

"Nath, why are you angry?"

He felt for her arms and gripped them above the elbows. "I'll tell you. I can't stand to be called a liar."

"Who called you that? Me?"

"Twice. Once when I said Tibby was gone from my thoughts, and again when I told you——"

"Go on."

"Aw, Meg, what's the use? A man can't squeeze his heart dry more'n once, not to somebody who won't listen and don't give a damn."

She dropped the flashlight and pressed against him, forcing his arms to go around her. "I do! I do! I guess I've loved you from the first day you came to Yocum Farm. I thought it was silly and knew it was wicked. I kept telling myself to quit, but I never have, never for a single minute. Now it's your turn, Nath; if you don't believe me, I'll die."

He acted like one stunned. "It's all right then."

She lifted her face with a funny gasp, half laugh and

half sigh. "Oh, you! Of course it is. For always. For ever and ever."

He found her lips, but it wasn't like kissing; it was something deeper, as locked as two streams that flow into one. He didn't have to tell her that they must hurry; even their thoughts went hand in hand. They crashed through the brush into the lane and trotted all the way home. Nath went straight to the phone.

"This is Nath Storm, sheriff, out to Yocum's. Didn't Doc Byrne ——"

"I know, I know!" broke in the sheriff impatiently. "Told me five minutes ago. Went to sleep in his car. More things happening to once! Rip Rinton's truck stole, his gal gone, and now you with one of them Barrens murders."

"Rinton's truck!" cried Nath. "When was it stole?"

"Nobody never noticed it was gone till they started looking for the gal round dinnertime today."

"Say," said Nath, "yesterday noon Rip's truck went by my place on Friesburg Pike. Teller Truman was driving. Had a girl with him I couldn't make out. Shouldn't wonder it was Tibby."

"How?" shouted the sheriff. "How's that again?"

"You heard me," said Nath, "and there's plenty more I got to show and tell out here to Yocum's."

"Wait there; I'm on my way," said the sheriff, and hung up.

Pete's hands gripped the arms of his chair and his little eyes began to bulge like marbles. "Huh!" he puffed. "Guess I'm ready as ever I was."

"You?" cried Nath. "Aw, heck, what you got to do with it? Nothing."

The sheriff made record time. Nath told him his story

rapidly, leaving out nothing. How he'd been knocked into the tarn one night and clubbed the next. The strange furrow meandering through the Barrens. The Red House. Meg's broken leg. Teller's affair with Tibby. The Rinton truck heading up the Friesburg Pike. Lot shot. Rumble rushing to his death. It all tied in, adding up to a hidden still as sure as two and two makes four.

"Fine, Nath," said the sheriff. "Let me at that phone."

"Wait a bit," said Nath. "Nearest a truck could come to the Red House would be a mile. Wherever it went, it can't be there."

"Think so?" said the sheriff. "Listen, whatever goes in has got to come out, don't it? We've checked the ferry and the Camden bridge. No soap. Now we've had a stop order on that truck since noon today and it ain't been heard from yet. You bet your way, I'll bet mine." He went to the phone and called the Rintons' number. "Troopers there?"

"Three on 'em," answered Mr. Rinton. "Any news, sheriff?"

"Nothing to count on yet. Get me the corporal." There was scarcely a pause. "Corporal? I'm over to Yocum's. Listen. One of ye beat it out the Friesburg Pike, cut across to the County Road, down to the village and back to Rinton's. Other two do it t'other way round, and don't quit with just one trip. Make it fast and keep going. Look for a truck running without lights. . . . Yep, the Rinton truck. That's all."

"Wasting time," rumbled Pete.

"How?" said the sheriff.

"Never denied it and don't intend to now," said Pete.

"Hush your noise!" whispered Ellen sharply.

Pete gave a puff that sent his beard and mustache into a

swirl, startling the sheriff, and his eyes began to glare. "The Red House. Elspeth hanging. Happen they hadn't of changed the law, Elspeth could tell me how hanging feels."

The sheriff glanced around, bewildered. "What's the old coot talking about?"

"He's dreaming," said Nath with a nervous laugh. "Dreams about the Red House; how it jumps from one place to another. A jumpity stone house, here today and gone tomorrow."

"Dreaming?" snorted Pete. "Ask Meg's leg! Ask Lot!"

Lottie rushed in from outside. "Broth, Ellen!" she cried. "Give me some broth! My boy's come to!"

XVII

IT WAS past noon before Reds ordered Tibby to climb out and stand ready to block. She woke to a shock. While she had been half sleeping, her subconscious mind had been at work, and now it handed her a fairly accurate picture. Reds was a moonshiner and a killer. The barrels contained liquor, and all Teller had wanted from the start was to gyp her into furnishing her father's truck. Where were they going? Would they take her with them? Of course they would; they'd have to. Her teeth chattered. But surely somewhere they'd stop or meet a car, and that's when she'd be ready to jump. The truck surged up and out; she blocked the rear wheels. A change came over Reds. Inside him still raged a caged beast; outside he had turned calm.

"Time for hurry's past," he muttered.

"How so?" asked Teller.

"Half the day's gone, ain't it? Up to about now, the gal's

folks been thinking she's tangled with a mired truck. But come noon and no gal, what happens? They start a holler."

Tellers' jaw dropped and he swallowed hard before he spoke. "Tib didn't tell about no mired truck. No call to. Up to her coming away at sunup this morning, nobody's noted it was gone."

Red's head jerked back as if a fist had jolted his chin. His yellow eyes turned bloodshot, but danger crowded all thought of a showdown from his mind. Too much was pointing his way—a girl's broken leg, a man shot, a dog torn apart, but not quite killed. Now this truck—known to be stolen, not just borrowed for a joy ride. It made a heck of a difference.

"We got to break outta here in a hurry," he decided aloud, "then hide till dark. No use trying for no ferry. Come dark, we'll run blind down the County Road, out through Muttonhead Wood, take to the Barrens agin, dodge Canton and slip down the wrong side of Stow Creek to Highjacker Landing. Nobody goes there no more. We'll bury the truck under marsh hay and git us a boat."

"Dark's far off," said Teller dubiously; "won't fall till eight." They worked feverishly, and at last the casks were snugged under the tarpaulin as before. "Want I should drive?"

"No," said Reds; "you tend to the gal. Happen her jaw moves, slam it shut. Got them bonds?"

"Yeah, I got 'em."

Wedged between the two of them, Tibby would have gone sick if it hadn't been for fright. She stared in terror as the truck negotiated the spider bridges, but the wide cripple with its corduroy bed turned out to be worse. The saplings gave unevenly under the heavy load. The truck careened like a boat at sea, and barely missed disaster. It clawed its way out and climbed to the firm ground under the jack pines. A laugh can turn into an ache in your throat. Here was where she had last dreamed of love—with Teller! Reds turned away from the Friesburg Pike and zigzagged through one wood road after another. When the forest thinned ahead in a straight line cut by telephone poles, he stopped, cramped the wheel and backed well out of sight behind a screen of bushes.

"Now we can sleep," he said, "turn by turn. Me first."

"Teller, please," gulped Tibby, "I'm going to be sick. Can't I sit on the outside?"

He let her change places, but kept an arm around her. She nodded, drowsed and pretended to sleep. Her teeth ached from chattering, all her body ached. Those high telephone poles marked the County Road, where a car might pass at any moment. If only, if only —— But the arm around her never slackened. No comfort to it, no more thrill than an iron bar. What would become of her? Tonight? Tomorrow? Newspaper headlines, making the worst of the story. The faces of her friends, all the girls she had queened it over or so long. The whispering, the snickering. She looked up at the sky in her desperation; it was leaden and turning black. Reds was sleeping soundly, hunched over the wheel. Teller let the twilight pass before he nudged him.

"Dark," he murmured.

Reds started the motor and let it idle to be sure it wouldn't stall. He eased in the gears. The truck crept out to the highway and headed north. No lights. Slow. Only the telephone poles to mark the way. The County Road stretches five miles without a curve, but something else takes the place of curves—undulations. You can see the headlights of a car far ahead and lose them six times before they come abreast. Reds saw a double flash in the distance, and so did Tibby. She thought she kept icy still, yet Teller's arm knew exactly what was happening inside her—heart starting to pound, all her muscles tensing, her mind dodging this way and that faster than her eyes. Like a giant crab, his hand sidled up from her waist and settled around her throat.

Reds saw the flash again and didn't worry. But the third time it leaped into view, it stabbed clean through his brain—the two lights weren't side by side; they were angled, one behind the other. He had counted on plenty of time to hide again, but these lights were coming too fast. Motorbikes. Troopers? Jail. The hot seat. What chance ahead? No road to the left and only one to the right, three dips away. Not a road—a lane, the narrow entrance to Yocum Farm. What good was that? Jail—you'll burn! The tarn! Escape! Hell, let the motorbikes come, the faster the better! He drew up on the shoulder as far to the side as he dared, motor still running, clutch and brake stamped flat. The lights blazed over the nearest rise, the bikes tore by. Troopers, damn 'em! Had they missed the dark blob of the truck? He had an instant of hope. It died, murdered by the screech of smoking tires, the popping of backfire and a stifled scream from Tibby.

"Throw her out! he yelled, letting up clutch and brake. "Throw the gal out!"

Teller jammed his elbow down on the door latch and sent Tibby headlong into the bushes. Unhurt, she turned and crawled out on her hands and knees; all fear forgotten, she was as mad as a soused cat. Already the truck had roared out of sight, but from behind her came another roar. She scrambled to her feet and waved frantically. The troopers slowed almost to a stop, feet dragging, their motors still making a din.

"Go after them!" she screamed. "Muttonhead Wood! Through Muttonhead!"

With the telephone poles to give him a line, Reds drove at full speed. Three dips, only three. On the first rise his eyes flicked to the mirror. Nothing. On the second they caught the headlights coming. They disappeared. This was it, this was his last and only chance. He slammed down both feet and skidded at right angle to the Yocum Farm lane. Shutting off the motor, he listened. The motor-bikes swept by at eighty miles an hour.

"Now what?" gasped Teller. "Know where you be?"

"Sure do," said Reds, snapping on the headlights and starting up the lane.

"Yocum Farm and no road out."

"Only one," said Reds. "Fix yourself to swim."

"S-swim?" stammered Teller. "What you aiming to do?"

"Slam truck and load into Yocum's marl-pit pond. Swim across. Hit for the marshes and keep going. Live awhile longer."

"Lose all our stuff?'" yammered Teller.

"Shut your fool mouth! How long afore those guys'll be back? What price your hide and mine? You want to burn?"

As the truck turned to pass through the drawgate, the reflection of its headlights flickered across the ceiling of the Yocum kitchen. Nobody noticed except Pete. He swelled like a puffin, and purple started to flood beneath his snow-white beard. His eyes took on their fish-scale glaze, but blind as they were, he managed to stagger from his chair and go blundering into the hall. Everybody with the exception of the sheriff thought he was heading for bed until they heard the front door open. That wasn't all they heard; the Rinton truck was in the act of passing. More, they heard more.

"Drive right around!" shrieked Pete with a wild sweep of his arm. "Drive right around and in!"

Steadying himself against the side of the house, he followed the truck as fast as he could toddle. Nath, Ellen, Meg and Lottie came streaming out, the sheriff last. Turning the corner, Pete went straight for the ramp while the truck had to make a wide turn. Reds gripped the wheel with one hand, holding the door on his side open with the other.

"Ready?" he shouted. "Here goes all!"

"Keep her straight!" yelled Teller. "Straight, damn you!"

The front wheels pitched over the crest in line, but when the rear tires hit the moss, they mashed it into slippery slime and the truck went into a pinwheel whirl. Everybody forgot Pete. Cries. Screams. The spinning truck wasn't spiraling toward the tarn; it was following the banking of the ramp.

Like flapping ears, Reds hung out one door, Teller out the other. When the truck hit the level, it scurried backward and crashed through the rotten icehouse doors. It sank into twelve feet of ooze, rear down, upright, only its headlights out and blazing. Teller falling into the ooze. Too thick to swim, too thin to tread. One arm straight up, reaching, sinking, gone! But not Reds—like a mighty tarantula, he lay sprawled face up across two slimy blackened beams.

Pete tripped as he reached the top of the ramp. He didn't pitch headlong, he became a rolling ball, governed by the same banking that had determined the course of the truck. Only the sill of the icehouse saved him. It caught his heels and fetched him standing. He turned young in his mind. He was a boy, teetering on the balls of his feet at the end of a diving board. With Nath and the sheriff in the lead, the rest came slithering down. The glare inside the icehouse amazed them; it couldn't be! Pete tipped forward, timing himself, fists hammering the air like somebody leading a band.

"Got ye, Hube!" he shrilled. "One hand—only one!"

"Pete!" screamed Ellen. "It ain't Hube! Pete!"

He hurtled forward and down. His right hand found Reds Truman's throat, his fingers snapped shut. The monstrous ball of him swung like a spider from a thread. Reds' strength could have matched the strain if the beams hadn't been oily with mold and decay. Hands and legs began to slip. Slow at first, then with a rush. A splash. A sickening gulp as the ooze licked its lips, slicked, grew still. Nath made a movement as if to leap. The sheriff seized him by the collar and yanked him back.

"You crazy? What good?"

The two of them stood staring into the icehouse, still ablaze with light. Slowly, things that long since had lost their form took on meaning. The gangrenous stubs of half-sawed joists. A tilted bit of floor. Strips of broken harness. The neck bones and skull of a horse, hung by his own collar. A tangle that could be the struts of a surrey. A spokeless wheel, speared over a jagged beam.

"Yeah," said the sheriff, "yeah. Seal it over with concrete and what have you got?"

"What?" asked Nath dumbly.

"A septic tank, same as it's been for fifty year. Here lies Hubert Snell, Reds Truman, Teller Truman, Pete——" He broke off. "Hell!"

"What?" repeated Nath.

"The Rinton girl—her folks'll want her out."

Nath felt sick, and so did Meg. They couldn't remember climbing the ramp; nobody could. They stood around in a group within the dim light from the window, not knowing what to do, uncertain where to go. The chug of a motor-bike hammered at their ears, but nobody seemed to hear it. Even the wide beam of the headlight caught them as still as figures done in wax. The trooper skidded to a stop.

"Hey, sheriff," he called. "Did a truck drive in here?"

"Sure did," said the sheriff, waking from his daze. "You boys don't have to trouble no more, only to go tell Rip Rinton."

"Tell him what?" barked the trooper.

"Truck's sunk and all in it drowned, including his girl."

"Tib?" laughed the trooper. "Not her, she ain't! She's a mile up the County Road, bawling her head off for you to come ride her home."

"Show the way," said the sheriff, making for his car.

Like a cork released from way down, Nath's heart bobbed up and up. Meg gave a great sigh. Ellen laughed, then sank on the edge of the porch and buried her face in her hands.

"Pete," she sobbed, "my brother! The boy you were! Strong! Gay! Long ago I killed you—long ago!"

"Rejoice!" called Lottie in a clear strong voice. "Would you weep for a lifted curse?" She turned toward the cabin, her face raised to the racing clouds, her arms spread wide.

"Shine, moon, shine and smile for the debt that's paid! Shine out! Laugh! Let dead folks lie, let live folks live! You hear me, Lot? Rise and sing!"

Meg looked up too. Her mouth opened and closed. That old moon, it was doing just as Lottie had ordered! One edge of it smiled from out a cloud, then the whole of it laughed. She didn't know whether she took Nath's hand or he hers. They walked out into the moonlight and stood as they had stood on that night of terror long ago. Only that time they had been separate, each alone in a trap; now they were as one. All of Yocum Farm lay displayed, its rugged disorder softened by night. Nath drew a quivering breath.

"What are you thinking?" murmured Meg.

"I'm thinking there's a load of work to do," said Nath, "but it's you and I can do it. Some folks build a house and it ties them together. We've got a heap more than that to build. A new world, starting from scratch. It's going to take us all life long."

"No time to be in love, Nath?"

He cupped her chin in his hands, tilted up her face and lost his eyes in hers. "Plenty, Meg."

THE END

Made in the USA
Middletown, DE
05 March 2021

34853881R00094